MOSTLY FICTION

ALSO BY THE AUTHOR

The Family Guide to Psychiatric Hospitalization (2025)
Johns Hopkins University Press, Baltimore, Maryland

MOSTLY FICTION

STORIES BY A SECOND GENERATION HOLOCAUST SURVIVOR

MARK J. RUSS

REGENT PRESS
Berkeley, California

[Paperback]
ISBN 10: 1-58790-725-9
ISBN 13: 978-1-58790-725-8

[E-Book]
ISBN 10: 1-58790-726-7
ISBN 13: 978-1-58790-726-5

Library of Congress Control Number: *forthcoming*

Book cover concept generated by ChatGPT,
finalized by the author.

Manufactured in the U.S.A.
REGENT PRESS
Berkeley, California
www.regentpress.net

To Yosl and Dora Russ
May their memories be a blessing

Contents

Acknowledgements

I do not think it would have occurred to anyone to encourage me to begin writing short stories late in life. It was not how people saw me and few knew of my holding the esteemed title of Editor-in-Chief of the Mirror, the oldest high school literary magazine in the United States (Central High School of Philadelphia). Even fewer people knew or cared that I had won several high school literary prizes and started my college career as an English major. It was in college that I received my first D in English. I earned the D for a freshman English essay related to one of Chaucer's Canterbury Tales and it was well-deserved. I eventually changed my major to Biology but am grateful to my English advisor at Haverford College, Dr. James Ransom, for setting me on a proper path. I would also like to thank Dr. Sigurd Ackerman, of blessed memory, my most important mentor in Psychiatry. Sig taught me to how to think clearly about scientific and clinical questions and how to concisely put my thoughts down on paper. I am indebted to him for teaching me a skill that would support my academic career in Psychiatry for decades to come.

I would like to also thank two individuals with a more proximal influence on my short story writing, Dvora Rabino, and her loving husband, Dr. Herb Leventer. In addition to their enormously valued friendship, they have provided steadfast support for my short-story writing. Dvora, an attorney and talented fiction writer, served as my editor for every story in the collection. Although this was an informal arrangement, Dvora demonstrated her enormous skill in gently and lovingly critiquing every aspect of the work. The stories grew and improved because of her considerable efforts. Herb, a professor of medical ethics and author of numerous essays and academic papers, likewise, provided unequivocal support and encouragement. His critical mind uncovered all sorts of themes in the stories, some intended, others not. I will always be grateful for their unconditional support and love. I would also like to thank Arthur Krystal, respected author, essayist, literary critic, and son of Holocaust survivors, for his astute and insightful editorial support and advice.

Finally, I want to thank my wife of forty-six years, Eve Edelman Russ, for her love, sharp eye, and wit, and my children, Ariel Russ, and Eli and Margo Russ, for their indulgence in listening to each new story, and reminding me that these stories are for them.

Introduction

On the occasion of my seventieth birthday, my wife gathered my writings from junior high school on, including many of the stories in this collection, and placed them in a loose-leaf binder. It was a very sweet and thoughtful thing to do. She wrote an introduction that she tucked into the transparent flap inside the binder cover. It was a lovely tribute. In an effort to be funny, she noted that the themes of my stories revolved around death and the Holocaust. I laughed when I read these words out loud, at which point my son added, "He can't help what he writes."

My son's point, true for all writers, I suppose, struck a chord, as did my wife's joke. The two themes, death and the Holocaust, of course, are strongly related. As a "child" of Holocaust survivors, I always knew the *shoah*, or as we referred to it in my home by its Yiddish name, the *khurbn* (destruction), was a silent onlooker in my family. I say onlooker and not intruder because the horror and despair were inseparably intertwined and could not be asked to leave. Any attempt to do so was a betrayal steeped in boundless guilt. So, the Holocaust remained a guest at our dinner table where I have no recollection of mundane conversation, or sometimes, conversation at all. *Khurbn* tales substituted for bedtime stories. Their ubiquity preempted the possibility of breathing freely, and their shadows promised a lifetime of darkness and limited possibilities. And my parents were lucky.

Pretending to be married, my parents fled east when the Nazis invaded Poland in September 1939. My father was thirty-two and my mother twenty-two. For the most part, it was the Jews who had the courage and physical ability to make it to the Soviet border who survived. The journey was dangerous, and the refugees were often caught in the crossfire between the Germans and the Soviets or were themselves the targets. Once in the Soviet Union, Jews like my parents had few choices. My father could be conscripted by the Red Army, or both could be sent to Siberia to work in labor camps. The Red Army was a likely death sentence. My parents chose the camps. They were taken from Bialystok by cattle car to the wilderness near the town of Kotlas, just south of the arctic circle. They struggled there for almost two years, felling trees in subzero conditions in the winter and enduring relentless mosquito swarms in the summers. Food and clothing were scarce. In 1941, they were "liberated" following enactment of the Sikorski-Mayski agreement between the Polish Government in Exile in England and the Soviet government, enabling the release of tens of thousands Polish "prisoners of war." Like many of their compatriots, my parents travelled by every imaginable conveyance to the south, eventually landing in Uzbekistan. They lived and worked on a collective farm and endured the same famine and hardships as the native population. To add to their misery, my father suffered a ruptured appendix and sepsis, yet miraculously survived thanks to a bottle of vodka used for anesthesia and an obliging Soviet army doctor. On at least one occasion, my mother came close to killing herself.

At the end of the war, my parents made their way to Lodz where they confirmed that only two of eighteen first-degree relatives survived the war. Realizing there was nothing left for them in Poland, they went to a displaced persons camp in Germany, and, with the help of the Joint Distribution Committee, moved to Paris a year later. They remained in Paris for a year where my father was able to find work as a knit worker in a textile factory. After Paris, they emigrated to Cuba where my father's sister and her husband had relocated before the war. They lived in a small town in Cuba, Jovellanos, several hours east of Havana, where they ran a general store and were the only Jews. It was there that my sister and I were born. After seven years, my family was able to enter the United States. We lived in Philadelphia where my mother's only surviving sibling lived. Without money or formal education, my parents worked in factories and eventually entered the lower middle class. English was their sixth language.

So, what does this have to do with me? Nothing and everything. Research interest in the intergenerational effects of the Holocaust began in the mid-sixties when the Canadian psychiatrist Vivian M. Rakoff, and colleagues reported high rates of psychological distress among children of Holocaust survivors. The notion of intergenerational transmission of trauma has received a great deal of attention since then and the model has been applied to many groups whose family legacies included severe and prolonged trauma. Although not all scientific studies have supported the validity of this phenomenon, there is sufficient support for the view that the effects of trauma in one generation can be passed on to the next. The mechanism of transmission has been studied as well and may include social learning within families, cultural elements within populations, and epigenetic factors.

What interests me about the themes of "death and the Holocaust," as my wife framed them, is that I did not set out to write any of the stories in this collection with those themes in mind. Rather, the stories emerged from a soup of experience, conscious and unconscious, and a need to write with purpose and from a perspective that felt honest and completely natural. The stories are a testament to my intimate relationship with an experience I never had, and childhood experiences I was only vaguely aware were neither average nor normal at the time they occurred. Unbeknownst to me, the lenses through which I saw the world in order to craft my stories were both created and warped by the fires of crematoria I had never seen.

I started writing short stories late in life, in my mid-sixties. I think I had three motives for doing so. First, I needed to work through emotions that were plaguing me, mostly related to loss near the end of my psychiatric career. Controlling the narrative of one's life through writing, as it were, is illusory, but if done well, it can be very useful. Psychologists might refer to this process as sublimation, channeling stressful or painful feelings and conflicts into creative endeavors. None of us can alter the narrative of the generations that preceded us, but for me, scholarship and writing became helpful ways to manage the many feelings stemming from my family's Holocaust experience and the experiences I encountered late in my own life. The stories helped quiet my mind.

The second reason for writing these stories was the pure joy of creation. I truly enjoyed the process of sitting down to write. It afforded me considerable pleasure and satisfaction to nurture an idea and bring it life.

Finally, I was interested in leaving my voice for my family. More than recordings and videos that will be available to them, these stories convey my authentic self, for better or for worse. Even more than my professional writing (I have many peer-reviewed papers in the psychiatric literature and a self-help book for families of loved ones with mental health problems), this short-story legacy fills me with pride and is how I want to be remembered by my children. The great Yiddish novelist and short story writer of the late 19th and early 20th centuries, Sholem Aleichem, included in his will that one of his stories should be read each year on the anniversary of his death. He was a supreme humorist and wanted his audience to remember him that way. I hope that reading one of these stories around a *yortsayt* candle each year will bring my children closer to the memory of me. I hope the candle's light will join with my words to embrace them and their descendants and allow my love to come shining through.

My wife was right. Even this introduction is about death and the Holocaust. I just can't help it.

Anya

Anya was the only resident at the Jacob Katz Manor with a *nom de guerre*. Born Brayndl Elenthartz in Warsaw near the intersection of Zamenhofa and Mila streets, not far from what became ground zero of the Warsaw Ghetto Uprising, Anya was not bred to be a heroine. Shy, soft-spoken, a blending-in-with-the-crowd kind of girl among her classmates at the *Gimnazjum*, Anya did not make a strong impression. Pretty enough with blue eyes behind wire-rimmed glasses and straight auburn hair, her high cheek bones made her face appear long and a bit sad. Her gaze was askew, seemingly unable to look people directly in the eye. At age nineteen in 1943, Anya was the perfect spy.

"You...fraulein...*dziewczyna!*" the German patrolman standing on a corner near the university on the Aryan side barked at Anya.

Anya continued walking, pretending the German was speaking to someone else. Feeling his stare tracking her, she stopped, breathed deeply, and coquettishly turned toward the soldier.

"What's in the satchel?" the German asked, pointing to the pouch and motioning Anya to reveal its contents. Anya, like most couriers in the Ghetto, carried a leather bag slung over one shoulder, the strap crossing her chest, subtly separating her breasts in the Polish "school-girl" fashion of the day.

"*Moja muzyka,*" Anya remarked without hesitation. "*Musyoka pianina.*" Anya was careful not to let on she understood German. Her courier pouch always contained legitimate university material to distract from whatever contraband may have been hidden in secret sections. Anya showed him her scores.

"No doubt that sentimental Chopin crap. Study some Wagner and you'll learn what real music is! Off with you to your filthy Chopin-loving, cur of a Polish boyfriend!" The German smirked, pleased with his small contribution to the war effort.

"Would you like some more bread, Anya?" the rotund server from Haiti at the assisted living facility asked, placing another slice of pumpernickel on her bread plate without waiting for an answer.

Anya recently turned eighty and needed a walker to

get around after her last stroke. She was a local celebrity of sorts, known as an off-color performer to the assisted living crowd. They also knew she was a "survivor" but did not know she had run tactical documents between the Warsaw Ghetto and the Polish underground.

"Yes, thank you, Marie," Anya replied in her barely noticeable Yiddish accent. "The bread is very good today," thinking how many such slices she could have smuggled into the Ghetto.

Anya was among the 500 prisoners who remained in Majdanek when it was liberated by the Soviets in July, 1944. Before her incarceration, she had been captured in Warsaw by the Gestapo after being outed by a Pole she had worked with in the underground. For reasons she never understood, she was deported to Majdanek as opposed to being shot on the spot.

"Why waste a good bullet?" she thought to herself.

"Maybe you'll perform for us later?" Marie asked.

In the decades before assisted living, Anya had developed a niche following for her one-woman performances. As a teen, she had become involved in some amateur Yiddish theater in Warsaw and showed some talent. Years after the war, she made it to Chicago where a distant relative lived and auditioned for the Compass Players, later to become Second City.

"Yes...maybe," Anya belatedly responded.

Anya finished her dinner and got up from the table.

She steadied herself on her walker and began the journey to her room. The faint fecal scent emanating from some of the rooms reminded her of walking through her barrack at Majdanek where the putrid smell of soiled hay-filled bunks overwhelmed her. Her wasted eighty-year-old frame weighed more than it did then. She reached the end of the first hallway where the daily activities were posted.

"How much bingo can a human take?" Anya mumbled to herself as she shook her head and continued to walk.

She turned left into a second corridor. Here, the floors were wood without carpeting so no one should trip. To dull the scraping sound of walkers on wood, the facility insisted that all such devices have tennis balls on their feet. Anya thought this was a stupid requirement that was mostly for the staff.

"None of the residents can hear anyway," Anya shared with her compatriots during a recent stand-up performance.

In another twenty yards, Anya arrived at the door to her room. It was open. She reached for the mezuzah hanging on the door jamb with her right hand and touched it lovingly as she entered.

Unlike other rooms in the assisted living facility, there were no photographs. No dead husbands or ungrateful children who never visited. No grandchildren to *kvel* over and show off. No one at all. Anya had only one relationship that meant anything to her; the relationship with her audience.

She sat down at the beige laminate desk and took out

lined paper from the top drawer. Without hesitation, she picked up her Bic pen and began to write.

"Sophie's Choice: Hermes or Prada!" Anya could hear the guffaws rolling onto the stage like a tidal wave.

"You're so dumb you think a crematorium is a place where dairy farmers hold meetings!" Anya burst out laughing so loudly the nearly deaf woman in the next room yelled "Shhh!"

The Nazi officer noticed Anya pacing outside the Ghetto gate near Nalewki Street.

"Are you looking for someone?" the officer suspiciously asked.

Anya was carrying a pouch full of secret documents. She did not feel anxious because such encounters were well-rehearsed.

"*Nie, kapitan.*" Anya knew he was only a sergeant.

"Well, there are only dirty Jews in there. Best stay away."

"Naturally...thank you, *kapitan*," Anya offered in her native Polish.

Anya's inner world was a jumble after the war when she learned she was utterly alone. She anticipated remaining so for the rest of her life. Her days were inhabited by reminders of all she had seen and smelled and heard during the dark years. Her nights were inhabited by Nazis. Factory smokestacks were crematoria. Blue striped awnings were prisoner uniforms. Approaching dogs caused her to freeze.

"Pretend you're a chicken...and Eugene, pretend you're a farmer, taken with your chicken. No words. Just facial expressions and body movements...that's it...like that...chase...chase..." Stan, a director at the improv studio, burst into laughter watching Anya tease the farmer.

"Brilliant! Anya, you're a riot! A natural!"

"I'm a shell," Anya thought but dare not say to Stan.

She half-smiled at the Soviet soldier on the day of liberation, not afraid of being raped again, knowing her breath and her body were repulsive.

"Thank you, Stan. You are very kind." Anya momentarily returned to character. "Does a chicken have lips?" Anya quipped, puckering her lips, and impishly raising her eyebrows.

"Jokes...I need more jokes for tonight," Anya said out loud to herself at her desk. "Why did the chicken cross the electrified fence?" Anya scratched her head. "I'll come up with the punch line later."

After about an hour of work, Anya put down her Bic pen and pushed her chair away from the desk with a sense of satisfaction. She put on her bathrobe and raggedy slippers, the costume she always wore for these gigs. Sheets of paper in hand, holding onto her walker, she made her way up the hallway from her room, turning left when she reached the activity board. This way led to the facility's living room where residents gathered after dinner. Small round tables scattered about gave the space the feel of a night club. At one end of the room was a small dais complete with microphone where invited performers occasionally came to entertain the residents of the Manor. A fellow resident helped Anya and her walker onto the low platform.

Anya's performances were mostly unannounced. The man who had helped Anya onto the dais switched on the microphone and turned off all the lights in the room except for a single overhead recessed light that cast an eerie shadow on her face. Anya tapped the microphone to get everyone's attention.

"It's Anya...shh...quiet everybody," could be heard from someone in the crowd.

"Achtung!" another shouted, and suddenly heads turned toward the dais from all corners of the room with retorts of "Jawohl!" amidst raucous laughter, imitating how Anya typically began her shows. This display was followed by murmurs, and, ultimately, silence. All eyes were on Anya.

She glared at her audience and then looked down at her notes. A nervous laughter emanated from the crowd.

Anya was the last prisoner in the sewing shop at Majdanek on a rainy spring day in 1944. The other women had been sent back to their barracks.

"Take off your clothes. The Germans have laws against touching Jewish cows, but we Poles are not so fussy," the guard in charge demanded.

Anya, terrified, stepped out of her clothes and out of her body. As the guard pinned her to the floor, the foul odor of what passed for vodka at that time swept across her face. She closed her eyes and was back in Warsaw, transforming the smell of alcohol to that of her fine leather satchel. And then it was over.

Anya started. "So, a rabbi and an SS officer walk into a bar..." The audience waited and waited and then exploded in laughter as she delivered the punchline.

"More...more..." they screamed.

"Picture a Jewish Abbott and Costello...They meet in Treblinka." The crowd soaked in the intro to what they knew would be a great bit.

"Who's on first?" a man cried out.

"No, no, no..." Anya shouted at the heckler. "That's Abbott and Costello in Bergen-Belsen!" The audience erupted.

The heckler persisted. "Tell us the Bergen-Belsen version!"

Anya pointed directly at the man who clearly had too much to drink with dinner. "Maybe another time."

"Come on everyone...We want Bergen-Belsen!" The heckler tried to stir up the residents and staff.

"That's enough out of you, Mr. Himmler!" Anya knew how to manage hecklers and not give them the upper hand.

"Then show us your tits!"

Anya smiled at the man in a way that signaled he had

crossed a line. Without uttering a word, she removed the Glock 19 which she always carried in her bathrobe pocket just in case and pointed it at the heckler.

A collective gasp arose from the audience, followed by a horrified silence.

Anya looked through the man who had behaved so rudely, her gaze no longer askew, and slowly pulled the trigger.

Click. Then nothing. The audience was motionless, frozen in place.

"Why waste a good bullet?" she said with perfect timing.

The audience roared.

The Doily

Thomas stood dumbfounded before the sepia photograph which hung in the living room of the agriturismo near Agrigento where he and Harriet were staying. The matronly innkeeper, her gray hair in an untidy bun and a faint trail of overly ripe Sicilian pecorino wafting behind her, approached them.

"Giuseppe Giordano. My great uncle. Difficult to explain. I try. It is lighter...eh...easier...easier to say what you have not seen than to say what you see.'"

Thomas tried to digest her words through her thick accent.

"The Son of Man," Harriet interjected, invoking Magritte.

"Yeah, without the apple. You can sort of see his face."

Thomas turned toward the old woman. "Can you tell

Originally published in Sortes, December, 2022

us more about the photograph? Why is it the only one on the wall like that?" Giuseppe's photograph was the last in a series of individual family portraits. Judging from their clothes, they all lived around the same time.

"The mask means the face is not seen. But the holes in la merletto say it is seen." The gray-haired proprietor said no more about her great uncle, making a quick zipper motion across her lips.

The object of Thomas' attention was a butterfly-shaped, loosely crocheted, white lace doily. Pressed between the protective glass and the photograph underneath, it partially obscured the face of a young man with a broad forehead and closely cropped beard. His eyes peered through the fenestrations of the delicate fabric. Thomas found the effect eerie, his imagination, like the doily, trapped behind the glass.

Thomas and Harriet wished the old woman a good evening and walked up the narrow staircase to their own two small rooms, passing old photographs of the Greek temples of Agrigento.

"Harriet, I would like to stay here a little while longer," Thomas declared but was really asking for permission. They were travelling through Sicily and had allotted only a day to see the local sights. "I want to understand what that crazy doily thing is about."

"The innkeeper turn you on?"

"She's old enough to be my grandmother."

Harriet smiled wryly but would not relent. "Uh huh..."

Thomas, a well-regarded feature writer for the Baltimore Sun in his late thirties, was prone to marital wanderings. The therapist whom he finally agreed to see with Harriet after the most recent indiscretion suggested an extended vacation might help. The itinerary and upper hand belonged to Harriet.

"Come on, what do you say? Aren't you just a little curious?"

"Alright. Two more days. But it better be good."

Harriet now took a leisurely shower, playing a little with the handheld spray head. When she returned to the bedroom, Thomas was already snoring.

Thomas awoke early the next morning and opened his laptop before brushing his teeth. He googled "doily," but drew a blank.

"Harriet, this city must have a library. Maybe in the university."

He showered, he shaved, he dressed and grabbed a cup of coffee and a roll from the breakfast spread the innkeeper had set out. Harriet was still in bed as he went out. A taxi had just dropped off a guest at the inn. Thomas hopped in and asked to be taken to the Universita Agrigento.

It was about five kilometers from the agriturismo. He paid the driver and stood before the library, an unimpressive two-story building that looked like a warehouse.

There was only one librarian, a young, dark-haired

woman whose hair almost reached the small of her back. As he told her about the photograph, he couldn't help sneaking glances. She was striking-looking, petite, wearing very tight jeans.

"I must say I never heard such a custom," confessed the librarian, clearly intrigued by the question, and a little by Thomas. "I research in one day."

"Thank you." Thomas turned to leave. "How will I find you tomorrow?"

"Alessia. Everyone here knows me."

Excited at returning to the library, Thomas, foregoing a taxi, jogged past the giardino botanico and the archeological museum. An hour later he was back at the agriturismo.

Thomas and Harriet spent the day touring the Valley of the Temples. Surrounded by the splendor of ancient Greek edifices, Thomas was able to let go of the photograph, at least for a few hours.

That evening at dinner, he wondered out loud, "Maybe I can turn this doily thing it into a piece for the paper."

Harriet's attention was focused on the illuminated temples that could be clearly seen from the restaurant patio. "Sure, why not?" she said. "If it pans out."

During dessert, Thomas paused between bites of his pistachio cannoli. "I am working with a librarian. She is helping me out."

He waited for the expected comeback, but none came.

The next morning, Thomas returned to the library and

found Alessia. She was wearing red-orange lipstick and brown mascara, a white button-down shirt, a black pencil skirt and matching black heels without stockings.

"No good," Alessia reported.

Seeing his disappointment, she added "I have one more idea. Come."

Together they walked the craggy streets lined with cheese shops, wine bars, and souvenir stores with miniature Greek temple replicas in the window. Politely stopping every man or woman who looked older than sixty, they met with many "prego... prego," usually accompanied by head shakes and shrugged shoulders.

After two hours, Thomas thanked Alessia. They shook hands rather formally, but she seemed in no hurry to let go.

"I'm sorry we couldn't find anything," he said, thinking he was now twice sorry.

"I, too," she said.

He was afraid to say anything else, so she turned and walked away. He watched her until she was out of sight. He walked five kilometers back to the agritourismo, but the spring in his step was gone. Was the lace doily a weird convention or simply an idiosyncrasy of the Giordano family?

He found Harriet reading on the balcony of their bedroom.

She barely looked up when he stooped and gave her a kiss. "Do you want to do something this afternoon?" she asked.

"Sure," he said. "Let me shower and change."

But instead of undressing, he went to the living room, opened his laptop, and again googled "doily." So many entries, so many images, but nothing about photographs. He kept scrolling- -- and there it was, many pages later: "doily," in a poem by someone named Elizabeth Bishop. It was called "The Filling Station." He found it and read it and read it again. He wasn't sure what the poet was trying to say, but the same lines kept drawing him back:

> *(Embroidered in daisy stitch*
> *with marguerites, I think,*
> *and heavy with gray crochet.)*
> *Somebody embroidered the doily.*

Grabbing the laptop, he rushed back to the bedroom.

"Listen to this," he said, trying to control his voice. "It's from a poem. Listen: 'Why, oh why, the doily?'"

"My question exactly!" And this: 'Somebody embroidered the doily.' Do you see? Whoever inserted the doily made the doily. The lace concealed what dare not be seen. Someone loved him deeply; it's there between the, you know, the openings in the lace."

"Who loved him?" Harriet asked, not bothering to look up from her book.

"The doily maker!"

Harriet stifled a yawn. "You promised we would be

leaving today."

"Just a few more hours," Thomas pleaded. Thomas rushed back to the library by taxi where he found Alessia helping a tall young man wearing a university futbol jersey at the circulation desk.

Thomas, shifting from foot to foot, waited for the young man to leave. He hurriedly explained his new plan of attack; learn as much as they could about Giuseppe Giordano and follow his story.

"We can start by searching baptism records, marriage documents, census reports," Alessia offered. She began to stride toward the reference section, motioning for him to follow. Suddenly, she stopped. "No. This way."

Thomas followed Alessia down a set of stairs and through the dark stacks. The air was heavy with the smell of old books. Alessia pulled a large volume off the shelf, a provincial history, and ran her finger down the index.

"I found something." She haltingly translated as she read. "Giuseppe was the son of a wealthy landowner whose family could be traced to the time of Bourbon rule in the Province of Agrigento."

In a section of the stacks devoted to periodicals, she then found an article in the newspaper, Giornale Di Sicilia, published in May 1919. It revealed that Giuseppe Giordano's father and Giuseppe after him became "men of honor," their clan joining another and forming a much respected and feared "family."

"Cosa Nostra," remarked Thomas.

Alessia nodded. She found an account of the younger Giordano's life and death toward the end of the same article. Skimming the piece, the librarian paraphrased as she translated. "It appears the young Giuseppe rose quickly in the ranks of the Cosa Nostra both because of his cleverness and brutality. He died a young man, in his thirties."

Reading directly now while translating, "'Although how he died...was not known, there was a rumor... he was kidnapped...and executed.'" Alessia paused and looked up at Thomas momentarily. "'He broke the rule, no...the code, of proper conduct. He loved the wife of his brother.'"

"Grazie." Thomas uttered softly, thinking for a moment to take advantage of the darkness.

"You are very welcome. Prego." Alessia awkwardly moved past Thomas, returning to the main room with the circulation desk. She accompanied Thomas outside the library and into the harsh afternoon light. They said their final goodbyes.

Thomas walked down the now familiar block where the library stood and caught the librarian watching him as he turned the corner.

He returned to the agriturismo and found Harriet napping on the tufted chaise lounge in their bedroom. Thomas approached her quietly and gently kissed her forehead.

"Another tryst with the sexy librarian?" Harriet muttered, slowly opening her eyes.

"Harriet don't be silly. She was helping me with my research. Come downstairs to the living room."

Thomas helped her up and led her by the hand as he retold the story of Giuseppe and how he died. They stopped in front of the line of photographs. Thomas now focused his attention on the portraits of the women.

"There! Look. The picture next to Giuseppe." It showed a woman in a long-sleeved, high-collared black dress with a simple crucifix necklace. She was sitting on a winged back chair, in partial profile. He grasped Harriet's arm and pointed out the fuzzy image of an unfinished doily on the woman's lap.

"That's her," remarked Thomas. "The doily maker, the lover. The truth seen could not be unseen!"

Thomas held Harriet more tightly. "Do you see?"

"Yes, Thomas. I see." Harriet said. She gently pulled away from his grasp. "Thomas, I am leaving you."

Thomas' face went white.

"This isn't working."

"I know." Thomas glanced again at the photograph of Giuseppe and finally understood its hold on him.

"Nothing happened," he murmured, but he knew it was too late.

The innkeeper, surreptitiously observing the couple from the corner of the room, cleared her throat to let them know she was there, then returned to her delicate crocheting. The thread was blue, not gray.

The Green Elephant

When I realized the green ceramic elephant wasn't missing after all, I could breathe.

Just a few inches high, it had stood on my mother's dresser for as long as I could remember. I loved running my fingertips over its smooth, cool glaze. The "Japan" stamp on its underside added to its exotic mystique; I was unaware of its mass-produced souvenir provenance.

I never learned how my parents acquired the elephant nor its appeal to them. They were certainly not collectors and had never been to Japan, although as refugees of the Holocaust, they had been almost everywhere else. I knew this fragile pachyderm could not have accompanied them

Originally published in Sortes, March, 2024

during the war nor in the rootless years that followed. The ceramic, I surmised, was a kind of placeholder, a stand-in for objects of real value they hoped would come with in a new life in America, but never did.

"You're addicted to Philip Roth," Valerie exclaimed when she walked into the living room and saw a copy of The Patrimony in my lap, my feet on the ottoman, my eyes staring off.

"What were you thinking about?"

I suspected Valerie really didn't want to know.

I was about to make something up when Abie, our four your old, bounded down the steps and plopped himself into my lap. Philip Roth saved me from a direct hit.

"Can we go to the playground, Daddy?" Abie's speech was fluent and articulate.

"Let me just finish reading this page and we'll go." Abie insisted on immediate responses.

We set off for the playground near the elementary school, Abie skipping circles around me.

"Push me, Daddy. Push me fast!"

I grabbed the closest stanchion on the merry-go-round, its red chipped paint covering the dimpled steel platform. It creaked at first but settled into a worn hum as it picked up speed. Abie clenched the opposite stanchion, his mouth gaping and his back hunched over, bracing himself for a dizzying ride.

"Faster!"

I ran and pushed and pushed and ran and ran and pushed with all the strength I could muster. Exhausted, I finally let go. Like an oscillating quasar, Abie's shrieks of joy whooshed louder and softer within each revolution. I relished Abie's delight against the centrifugal force.

Abie jumped from the merry-go-round when the creaking sound returned, a sign it was safe to hop off. He climbed the stairs of the slide and skidded down, ran to the monkey bars where he hung by one arm and hooted "Oo oo oo," swung belly-down on the swings, and boomeranged to my side.

"Let's go, Daddy."

My thoughts had returned to the ridges in the elephant's glaze, smooth and cool.

"Let's go, Dad!" Abie was more insistent, already by the playground entrance gate.

When I realized he was no longer at my side, I followed quickly, not wanting him to approach the street without me. I gripped his hand tightly. When we were safely across, he ripped it free and ran ahead.

"How was the playground?"

"Daddy pushed me real fast, but I wasn't afraid. The merry-go-round is my favorite."

"Your son is a whirling Dervish. Not sure he would return in one piece."

"Oo oo!" Abie imitated a monkey again, scratching the armpit of his raised hand, and bolted up the stairs.

Valerie sat next to me on the sofa, our thighs touching. She grabbed my hand.

"It's good you took him out. He really enjoyed it. I'll do the chest PT tonight."

"I can do it. Give you a break. Besides, we both know I'm better at getting up the mucus."

"Did he wheeze in the playground?"

"Just a cough here and there. He was full of energy."

"That's good. But for how long?"

"One day at a time, Valerie." I released my hand from hers and stood up. "We'll give him the best life we can for as long as we can."

Now it was Valerie who was staring off at nothing.

Suddenly, Abie appeared, his hands behind his back.

"Daddy, I was playing monkey and it broke. It was an accident." Abie revealed two pieces of green ceramic, one in each hand. "Can we glue it together?"

Valerie looked at Abie, then me. Her eyes said she did not know who to console first.

"Sure," I said, without the slightest hint of conviction.

The Suicide Note

Henry ignored his pitch-black stools for a while until his denial surrendered to his better judgment. That defense of last resort faltered in the end and was replaced by humor, which allowed him to make an appointment to see his gastroenterologist for a colonoscopy. He planned to sing the first few lines of Michael Jackson's Thriller just as the propofol entered his vein. The fact that the joke was in bad taste would not deter him. He was sure the anesthesiologist, gastroenterologist, and nurse would crack up as he fell into that delicious sleep.

Unfortunately, the immediate onset of the propofol's magical effect precluded Henry's knowing for sure how his joke landed. He could not feel the camera snake its way into his anus, up through his rectum, chicane into

Originally published in The Minison Project, TMP Magazine, Issue 1, 2022

the sigmoid colon, and finally ascend into the ascending colon, where it abruptly stopped. Amidst the pink mucosa, occasional diverticula and rare fecal residual the tip of the colonoscope came face to face with a 5x8 cm mass. The tumor was irregular in every aspect, friable, and black in spots, where it was cannibalizing itself and the surrounding tissue. Prick it and it would bleed. The mystery of the melena was solved.

The juxtaposition of Henry's blissful post-propofol mental status made it both easier and harder to assimilate the dripping of words like "mass" and "tumor" from the doctor's mouth. Biopsy result few days staging surgery maybe temporary colostomy don't worry we'll be with you. All Henry could think about was his wife in the waiting room waiting to drive him home. Henry and Elsa had been married for thirty-five years. Although Henry was a competent and recently retired internist, he relied on Elsa to calm him when he felt anxious, even when he knew much more than her about the subject of his worry.

"It's cancer," he blurted out, half crying, half raging and entirely, "I told you so," as though that Pyrrhic victory could allow him to avoid the panic that was rapidly settling in. Henry wanted Elsa to make it better, but Henry learned at an early age that women cannot be counted on for this. He was accustomed to relying on himself in the final analysis.

"Let's hear what the doctors have to say. You're always

jumping to the worst case scenario," Elsa reminded Henry, her voice a mixture of desperation and irritation, and void of reassurance. The biopsy results came back in a few days: invasive adenocarcinoma with high-grade dysplasia.

Indeed, the doctors had a lot to say. They outlined a game plan that included staging the cancer, surgery, and a bunch of blood tests for genetic markers and other stuff. Henry dutifully listened and made appointments for blood draws, CT scans of the abdomen, pelvis and chest, with oral and IV contrast. The results were bad. Stage 4 colon cancer with metastases in the mesentery, liver, and lung. The genetic testing did not make Henry a good candidate for chemotherapy. The only good news was that Henry would not die with a colostomy. He would die with an end-to-end anastomosis of his ascending and sigmoid colon segments. Six months.

Six months to pack in that ski trip to the Swiss Alps he had always put off. Six months to finish his book with the working title, *My Life as a Prison Doctor*. Henry was used to imagining there would be time. So much so that he never learned to live each day. Six months was a room with four walls and without doors. No option but to slam into one no matter which way he turned.

Henry was numb, longing for a propofol drip. He could not get Thriller out of his head, even as he was contemplating suicide. Contemplating suicide was not a new experience for Henry. As he was growing up, he had often seen killing himself as the solution to a whole variety of his troubles, most of them extremely trivial in retrospect. But Henry had other tricks up his sleeve. Anticipation was one of Henry's most reliable defenses. He found planning for something way ahead of when it might harm him to be extremely helpful. This applied to preparing for a test in school or for the next hurricane. Coupled with magical thinking, he lived by "Henry's Rule," raising anticipation and worry to heretofore unknown heights of effectiveness. Henry was convinced that if he worried about some particular event happening or not happening, it wouldn't. The caveat, however, was that he really, really had to worry. And this he did because he was really, really gifted in this regard.

Henry realized, however, that "Henry's Rule" had its limitation and no amount of worry could prevent the current inevitable course of events. Therefore, he reasoned, suicide was back on the table. Although Henry was not big on making charts comparing pros and cons of options he was weighing, he made an exception in this case. Pros. In favor of suicide. Mastery and control. Henry would decide when, where and how he would die. Avoidance of pain. Henry could skip the months left him that would likely be filled with physical pain and/or the fogginess and constipation than would come with measures for pain relief. Avoidance of anxiety. This was the big one for Henry. Why torture himself with months of wondering what death would be like, what was on "the other side," and the panic of the final breath? And then there was the panic of false hope.

A formidable list, Henry thought. He put down his pen, rubbed his eyes, and considered that the rationale for ending his life by his own hand was staring him in the face. He could not immediately think of what could compete with these arguments. Somehow the difference between killing himself and being killed by this alien beast in his gut seemed inconsequential. Dead is dead.

Instead of writing up a list of cons, Henry decided to write a suicide note.

Dear Elsa,

By the time you read this note you will know that I am gone. I am very sorry to have to say goodbye this way, but I am quite sure you would have tried to stop me if I told you what I was planning to do.

Henry did not actually have a plan yet.

I feel stuck. I don't really know what to say. I picture you crying as you read this and that would make me sad except that I am already dead. Will I feel anything after I am dead? Neurons just sitting there, cold, and dumb, unable to talk to each other. Sort of how I feel now, Elsa. I loved you, of course. You were good to me. Thank you. That sounds so stupid. I want to say something meaningful...you know...memorable.

Even now that I am dead, I want to remember how warm you felt when I embraced you. You felt "like a little radiator," I used to say. I never understood how you managed that, warm, even when everything else seemed cold around us. And I want to remember your half-smile, looking at me from the corner of your eye, making us cheese omelets and turkey bacon on Sunday mornings. And how you clung to me, almost desperately, when we made love and how that let me know it was good. It wasn't always so wonderful, of course, and I know I caused you pain. I tried to be a good husband, but I know I could have done better. This letter isn't working. I wanted it to be better too, but here it is. I will miss you, Elsa. I am sorry for going this way, but the end was in sight anyway, so I hope you forgive me. I love you my sweet.

Henry was dissatisfied with his suicide note but decided it was good enough. He signed it "Love you forever, Henry," placed it in an envelope, sealed it with a lick of his tongue and hanged himself from the waste pipe in his basement. Thriller slipped from his lips between the gasps.

Elsa found the body that evening when she came home from work and Henry had not appeared for dinner. She was not completely surprised. She ran up the stairs of the basement and called 911, knowing it was too late but not knowing what else to do. The ambulance and police came, cut him down and brought him to a local hospital morgue, where he was stored in a refrigerated drawer. The police read the suicide note and interviewed Elsa who told them about Henry's Stage 4 colon cancer. They said it was not a case for the M.E., and they left.

Alone again, Elsa sat down with the note and read it over and over, looking for something she did not know.

Crumbs of Hope

Having unintentionally left his mother to die alone at Our Lady of Mercy several years before, Malcolm was determined to remain with his father until the end.

"The dialysis didn't do what we hoped. His heart is weakening and his lungs are filling with fluid." Dr. McArthur said as he gently patted Malcolm on the back. They watched the orderly push his eighty-eight-year-old father out of the ICU room he had occupied for three days and down the hall.

"He'll be in a single so you can have your privacy. We'll keep him comfortable."

Malcolm, a bachelor dermatologist in his fifties, unaccustomed to being in acute medical settings, nevertheless knew what was coming. He used a pay phone in the lobby

Originally published in *Jewish Fiction.net*, March, 2023

to call his sister at home. "Multiple organ failure... a day or two...morphine...MORPHINE......no, it won't make him better...it helps the sensation of drowning. Room 264. Flannery Pavilion."

Malcolm's sister arrived thirty minutes later having completed some errands that afternoon. She greeted Malcolm with a hug as she entered her father's room and inquired about his condition.

"No change."

The siblings sat on either side of the bed in silence, interrupted only by the sound of dinner trays being served to other patients down the hall.

"What's the plan for tonight?" Barbara asked.

"Why don't you go home, Barbara. Your kids will want you close by. It's been a long few days. I'll stay with him tonight." Malcolm, wearing a rarely used stethoscope he'd brought "just in case he needed it," glanced toward the nurse who'd been charting on a clip board at the foot of the bed.

"Would that be ok? If I stayed with him tonight? I can sleep in that chair," pointing to a green Naugahyde recliner in the corner of the room. The upholstery was frayed on the armrests and seat cushion, and there was a faint smell of cigarette smoke.

"I'll get you a pillow and blanket." The nurse's eyebrows were slightly furrowed over the bridge of her nose and the corners of her mouth drew downward.

"Thank you. There. It's settled. I'll see you in the morning, Barbara."

Barbara knelt by her father's bedside. Tears began streaming from her mascaraed eyes onto her cheeks.

"Tateshi...Daddy..." Barbara whispered. She was a few years older than Malcolm and always took care of their father, more so since their mother died. She kissed her father's forehead, squeezed his hand tightly, and left the room, blotting the blackness on her face with a Kleenex.

Moving gracefully, the nurse finished settling her patient in for the night. She raised the head of the Hill-Rom bed about thirty degrees, repositioned his pillow and carefully adjusted the oxygen prongs in his nostrils. Malcolm appreciated that she tenderly cared for his father, no differently than for a patient who was expected to live.

The little ball in the green oxygen flowmeter read 4 liters/minute. A Foley bag with scant dark urine hung from the side of his bed. An IV in the left arm provided access for the morphine that would be needed. That's all there was. Spartan trappings by hospital standards, and certainly bare compared to the ICU. No machines were beeping, just the machine that was his father, fading in and out of consciousness and breathing with effort.

"I'll be just down the hall in the nursing station if you need anything," the nurse offered, stopping at the door of the hospital room on her way out.

"Thank you. You and the entire staff have been terrific."

Realizing he had not eaten all day, Malcolm made his way to the first-floor coffee shop for his usual hospital meal, tuna on toast and a cherry coke. Even after days in Our Lady of Mercy, he could not help but notice the immaculately polished floors and strategically placed crucifixes along the walls. He ambled down the hall, bidding good evening to the staff and occasional nun.

"I'll have a tuna on toast...no...make it a BLT...and a cherry coke." Malcolm kept kosher at home, but gave himself permission to eat *treyf*, non-kosher food, when out in the world, including in his current surroundings. He found it curious that his parents, Holocaust survivors, who primarily spoke Yiddish and English with a thick Yiddish accent, felt comfortable in this supremely goyish environment. Having abandoned organized religion because "God abandoned us" in favor of a fervent secular, left-wing Jewish life, they were not particularly bothered by the Catholic accoutrements. *"Der* hospital is *cloyz* by and Dr. McArthur is a *mensch,"* his mother would say. Malcolm, for his part, was not ready to give up on God, but understood his parents' feelings.

"Well, at least I did not order a milk shake," he remarked to the heavyset waitress with "Jesus" tattooed on her forearm in elegant blue script complete with curlicues. Looking up at her rotund face, he knew she did not have a clue what he meant. Malcolm scarfed down his sandwich, finished his drink, stopped in the restroom, and returned to his father's room for the night.

His father's condition was unchanged except there were no longer any periods of consciousness, even brief ones. His eyes remained closed and he did not respond to questions. There were bursts of agonal breathing, a sure sign he was nearing the end, and not much urine in the Foley bag. Everything was shutting down.

After watching several hours of the Thursday evening line-up on NBC, Malcolm decided to shut down for the night as well. He turned off the lamp on the wall over his father's bed. The only other light in the room was a sliver coming from around the bedroom door which was left slightly ajar. He lay down on the Naugahyde recliner; it was more comfortable than he had imagined. Pulling the cotton hospital blanket up to his chin, he settled into a rather unencumbered slumber, comforted by the thought that he was just where he needed to be.

Malcolm was sleeping soundly for several hours when he was suddenly awakened by an utterance coming from his father's direction.

"GIB MIR KHOCH A SHTIKL HOF!"

Malcolm sprang up into a sitting position, now wide awake.

"What did you say?" Malcolm removed the blanket, jumped off the recliner and positioned himself at his father's bedside. "Did you really say 'Give me at least a crumb of hope?'"

He turned on the light over his father's bed and saw he was as unresponsive as before.

Feeling a need to check his condition further, Malcolm reflexively took up his stethoscope and listened to his father's heart and lungs. He heard the gurgling of fluid that was continuing to fill his lungs despite the infusions of morphine. His heart was another matter. Lob dub, lub dub, lob dub, lub dub...the heart sounds, while somewhat muffled, were stubbornly strong.

"A distinct S1 and S2," Malcolm thought. He strained to hear an S3, a sign of the heart failure he knew would kill his father, but could not discern a third sound.

"Dad...Popi...say again what you said. *Zog es nokh amol.*" Malcolm instinctively switched to Yiddish, magically thinking that might generate a response. Malcolm caressed his father's forehead, slightly moist with sweat, and gently combed his hair with his fingers, morphing between physician and son and back again.

"*Vos host gemeynt?* What did you mean?"

Malcolm decided his father's plea was real, caused by a delirium. His demand was nothing more than the meaningless output of an oxygen-deprived brain.

Yet, Malcolm was not satisfied with this explanation. His father's demand for hope seemed so lucid, so insistent. He let his thoughts wander through his father's tormented life for a clue to its meaning.

Was it the plea for hope of a frightened boy of six sent

to live with indifferent relatives after his father died in the Spanish flu pandemic in Poland?

Was it the plea for hope of a frantic young man fleeing the Nazis in 1939, barely outrunning the *Luftwaffe* raids?

Was it the plea for hope of a haggard man in Siberia in 1941, starving and freezing, forced to cut timber for his Soviet enslavers?

Was it the plea for hope of an emaciated carcass returning home from the East in search of his family only to learn he was the only survivor?

Or was it the plea for hope of an old dying man begging for one more morsel of life at the end?

Malcolm turned his father's words over and over in his head until they began to rotate faster, like some mirrored carnival spinning wheel. Slowing, as all such devices inevitably do, the pointer landed on the last option, leaving Malcolm staring at his own reflection. Feelings of guilt that Malcolm had tried to keep in check now flooded him.

"Did you really think I could do something to turn this thing around?" Malcolm's tone grew panicky and angry.

"I can't make everything better for you. I can't do life and death!" Now it was Malcolm who was pleading. His thoughts took him to a painful, familiar place.

Malcolm reached to turn off the light above his father, and as he did so, broke down, his face buried in his hands. His sobbing became uncontrollable, drowning out his father's labored breathing.

"There's nothing I can do," he repeated over and over again.

He cried in the dark for what felt like a very long time. Exhausted, his tears gradually subsided as fatigue set in and his attention shifted to the illuminated dial of his wrist watch. Two-o-seven... two-o-eight... two-o-nine... Malcolm unknowingly began to interpose his breaths in the widening silences between those of his father's.

"*Zorg zikh nisht, mayn zun.* Don't worry, my son. You did the best."

Malcolm could not tell for sure whether he was imagining what he heard. He looked up from his tear-soaked hands. His father's face, motionless and without expression, was partially illuminated by the light coming from the slightly cracked open door. He strained to absorb these words of reassurance from his father, just as he had strained to hear that abnormal heart sound that could not be appreciated but he knew had to be there.

Malcolm then realized he could no longer make out his father's breathing. Bending over, he placed the earbuds of his stethoscope in his ears and listened intently for heart sounds. There was no S1 and there was no S2. There could be no S3. He removed his stethoscope and placed it around his neck. His father was dead.

Spent, his eyes swollen from sobbing, Malcolm then saw an apparition hovering above the lifeless corpse. His father's soul, homeless and alone for the first time in eighty-eight years. It appeared to be swimming in the space just below the ceiling, lacking substance, but radiating brilliant, luminescent colors; now cobalt, now gold, in short-lived bursts. It reminded Malcolm of a squid that could instantaneously change color and camouflage itself in order to avoid danger. He gently motioned to the soul, conveying there was nothing here to fear, and coaxed it to descend. Malcolm removed his stethoscope from around his neck and replaced it with his father's arms.

The three embraced.

Malcolm, satisfied, strode from the room and down the immaculate hall to tell the nurse what had happened.

Old Man Smell

Max thought he awoke in his father's closet. His mother, long gone, had not been able to part with her husband's things. The closet lived on as a musty shrine for several years until Max finally forced her to call for the Goodwill truck.

As his semi-sleep state cleared, Max slowly realized it was he and not the closet that smelled. To make sure, he surveyed his body, cupping his hand over his nose as he moved between chest and underarm. He detected traces of sweat mixed with Old Spice and the faint odor left by skid marks from below.

"Damn bacteria start eating away at you long before you're dead," he murmured to himself.

Meg, his wife of forty years, had placed a lavender

Originally published in Jimson Weed, Spring, 2024

sachet in his very full underwear drawer, hoping that would eliminate what she thought was just the odor of rarely used, bottom-dwelling garments. This intervention had two unfortunate outcomes: it added a sickeningly sweet floral scent to the stale mix and it confirmed Max's fears of beginning to smell old like his father.

"It's a known fact that people smell 'old' on you before you do," Max lectured Meg at breakfast that morning. "That's just the way it is."

Meg looked at him, lips pursed and frowning, ready to change her expression at the slightest hint she was being put on.

"It's not like you stroke out and can't talk anymore or your knees hurt from arthritis. Old man smell just creeps up on you."

Meg always cackled at Max's jokes, declaring she was his best audience when others in the crowd merely chuckled.

"Max, I can't tell if you're kidding."

Meg stubbornly waited for a punchline that did not come.

Six months before, Max's boss had called him into his office.

"We've decided to restructure the department and we're going to be eliminating your position, Max. Thank you for all your contributions."

"Was that when the smell started but I couldn't tell?"

Max asked Meg, staring into his plate of eggs and par-tially-eaten toast. He wondered whether the telltale odor worked like a pheromone that triggers heartless behavior in bosses.

Not waiting for an answer, he pushed on.

"They told me I was an 'at-will' employee. That means they can fire you 'at will,' for any reason or for no reason." Retelling the story to Meg, Max's voice rose. "Now I'm just an 'at-will' human being."

Max took a half-hearted bite of his toast. An image of the dead, like sheep, passing under the staff of God, flowed into his awareness. He pictured God in shepherd garb counting and judging souls and determining their fates. Focused on "at will," he had not thought much of "God's will" until recently.

Meg had heard all this before. "Don't worry. Something will come up."

This dismissive reassurance was enough to dislodge Max from his absorption and the odd juxtaposition of God, his boss, and his future.

"Well, it won't be my penis." He tried to smile, but his lips refused to move.

"Never mind that," Meg quipped, trying to bolster his attempt to be funny.

But he did, he did mind it.

*

Max had not thought a lot about retiring before he was fired. But at sixty-six, having always worked for large accounting firms, retirement seemed inevitable. He earnestly tried to find something to do. He went online and read "10 Tips on Retirement" followed by "6 Mistakes People Make When They Retire," and then, "8 Reasons 65 Is the New 40."

He had "mourned the loss," taken "a good hard look at himself," and done all he could think to do to "write the new and exciting next chapter of his life."

Max wasn't good at next steps. There wasn't a musical instrument he had wanted to learn to play. To Meg's chagrin, he disliked travel, preferring to sleep in his own bed. He and Meg never had children, so there were no grandchildren to babysit. Max was an accountant. He liked the detail and the precision. He liked going to work. Little else appealed to him.

It wasn't long before Max began to feel depressed.

"Max, you can't lay around all day watching sports on TV. Let's at least go for a walk."

But Max wasn't just watching sports on TV. He was thinking about death, picturing himself lying in a casket. He imagined life might go on there, just in a more confined way.

"Max ... Max!" Meg was now almost yelling. "Look at me!"

"What? ... Sorry Meg, I was thinking about something."

"About what?"

"The smell."

"What smell?"

"My smell. In the coffin. You'll need to stock up on those lavender sachets." The anemic joke did not land. Meg no longer encouraged this type of humor.

"Max, stop talking like that. You've had a serious blow. It happens to lots of people. They get over it. So will you."

"Not the smell, Meg. The smell just gets worse and worse. You become the smell. You become shit."

Max could see in Meg's face that this was more than she expected and more than she could manage.

"Maybe you should see somebody. I can't stand seeing you like this. I love you."

"And I love you, Meg. I just can't stand the smell."

*

Months passed and Max's fingers, already thin, grew bonier. Not eating or sleeping well, he was shriveling. Every day was the same. Every hour or so he would stand up from the couch, walk down the hall toward the kitchen, occasionally tripping on the worn oriental runner, turn around, walk back up the hall, and return to the couch.

"Where should I go?" he repeated to himself as he ended each cycle and lay back down.

Meg overheard him. "Max, you have an appointment tomorrow with the psychologist I found."

Obediently, he went.

"Tell me more about the smell, Max," the therapist inquired.

"What about it?"

"Well, what comes to mind when you think about it?"

After a long pause, Max whispered, "Oh, I don't know ...deterioration, decay, death. The usual suspects." Max's irreverent humor was on life support.

"What else?"

Max did not respond.

"What else?" Dr. Harvey insisted.

The pause was longer this time.

"When I was young, I spent a few summers at a race-track near my home. Worked as a stable boy. Groomed the horses. Walked them, fed them, watered them. I loved it."

The word love sounded jarring to Max, but he went on.

"Loved every minute of it. The horses were beautiful: strong and willful. Real thoroughbreds."

Max stopped again, partly from fatigue, but mostly from wondering why he was talking about such an obscure memory.

"People asked me if I minded the stench, you know, from the hay and dung. I told them, not at all. I kind of liked it."

"What did you like about it?"

"The horses didn't mind it. Why should I?"

"Go on."

"It was their smell. Part of them. What made them alive, and fast. Kinda like the exhaust from a Maserati."

"You weren't disgusted?"

"Not at all. Just the opposite."

"And your smell?"

Max felt caught off guard and a little tricked.

"I'm at the end. Run down. You know." Max bowed his head.

"I don't know that at all. Seems to me, Max, when it comes to your smell, there may yet be a pony in that stable."

After another long pause, Max looked up, and then at his watch.

"Is it time?"

•

"How was your session, Max?"

Max returned to the couch, although its hold on him seemed less firm. He lay down and looked straight up at a meandering crack in the ceiling. Meg's face invaded his field of vision.

"Get up."

Max did not move.

"I said, get up. We're going out." Meg's tone was stern, but a half-smile signaled an unexpected playfulness.

"Out where?"

"Out. What difference does it make?"

Max sat up and looked at Meg. He had not realized she was already dressed to go. She wore a blood-red leather jacket with a matching belt tightly wrapped around her torso. The jacket accentuated her narrow waist and round hips. Her graying hair was cropped. Max thought she looked pretty, reminiscent of her appearance he found so appealing when they dated in their twenties.

Without saying a word, Max sat up and turned his body, so his feet touched the floor. Meg's energy was enough to lift him from the couch. He felt an urge to embrace her, a feeling he thought was gone forever.

"Where are we going?" Max's inflection revealed some interest in the answer.

This time, it was Meg who did not respond. Instead, she gently took Max's hand in hers and they walked into the briskness of the October day, overcast and welcoming. And Max took in the smell of leather emanating from Meg's jacket wafting above the pungent odor of fallen leaves in piles, some fresh, some burning in the distance.

Yosl and Henekh

My father, Yosl Russ, was born in 1907 in a shtetl 30 miles southeast of Warsaw called Kaluszyn (Kal-u-sheen). Kaluszyn, the Poles corrected my pronunciation to Kal-oo-shyn (I explained mine was the Jewish pronunciation), was a midsize commercial town that was on a major trade route between Warsaw and eastern Poland and Russia. My father was one of six children born to a poor family that dealt in the beer distributing business; they had a small tavern connected to their home. The family was observant like all others in the shtetl. Crisis struck the family when my father's father suddenly passed away in 1917, one of millions of victims of the Spanish flu pandemic. With no means of support, the family moved to Warsaw. My father was sent to live with an aunt at the age

Originally published in The Jewish Writing Project, March 7, 2022 of 10 and spent his teenage years performing housework and eventually learning to work in the knitting trade. He, like so many others in his poverty-stricken, working-class generation in Poland became radicalized, gave up religious observance, embraced a Jewish brand of socialism and internationalism, and went on to organize like-minded Jewish youth in Warsaw. He became active in the Jewish Labor Bund, the principal Jewish political party of his time and place, a Yiddishist, consistent with the Bund's tenets, and a leader in the party-affiliated sports and out-doors organization, *Morgenshtern*. The latter provided organized physical activity and an appreciation of the nat-ural world to slum-bound, impoverished Jewish working youth. He led "ski trips," hikes and other expeditions in the Carpathian Mountains and environs of Warsaw. It was in this context that he met my mother.

My parents never wanted to return to Poland after the war. They had escaped east to Bialystok and the Soviet Union in 1939, one step ahead of the German advance into Poland. They spent the next 18 months in a forced labor camp in Siberia cutting timber. The Sikorski-Mayski Agreement was struck in 1941 between the Soviet Union and Polish Government in exile in London, effectively lib-erating all Polish citizens held captive by the Soviets. My parents, like tens of thousands of other Polish Jews who had taken the same path, made their way south in a har-rowing journey through the Soviet heartland. They spent the remaining war years in Uzbekistan. After the war they briefly returned to Poland to see who had survived; all but one sibling on each side of the family perished. They lived in a German DP camp for a time, Paris for a year, and eventually immigrated to Cuba (where my sister and I were born), and finally, to Philadelphia.

This background is necessary to explain what happened when my wife and two adolescent children decided to visit Poland. Initially, the trip was planned as part of a larger Bar Mitzvah journey for my nephew's son that was to begin in Poland and end in Israel. Timing was such that we could only join my sister's family for the first part of the trip. I shared my parents' reservations with respect to visiting Poland. I imagined a land full of anti-Semites, denigrating me and insulting me on the streets of Warsaw. Although I had powerful trepidations about the trip, I remained curious about what it would be like. Part of me was drawn to travel there.

My father had a younger brother, Henekh. Growing up, I heard bits and pieces about his life. I heard that he was smart, quick-witted, passionate, and very energetic and capable. I also knew that he was very well thought of. My parents' friends, all Holocaust survivors, many of whom were bona fide heroes in the Warsaw Ghetto Uprising and partisans in the Polish forests, all knew him and held him in high esteem. He was one of them. As I grew older, I read some of the biographical sketches that had been written about him in Yiddish texts. Before the war he had been a leader in the young adult section of the Jewish Labor Bund, the *Tsukunft,* and served on the Bund's Warsaw central committee, a major achievement for someone so young. With the advent of the Internet and newly discovered references to him in a variety of books and documents, I learned more about him over the years. I learned that he had been an active member of the Jewish underground in the Warsaw Ghetto, and that he had been the co-editor of one the underground newspapers, *Yugnt Shtime,* preserved as part of Emanuel Ringelblum's Oneg Shabbat archives. He also authored a "diary" consisting of the proceedings of meetings and historical events related to the Bund in the Warsaw Ghetto, preserved in the YIVO Archives in New York. I learned that his infant son was killed during a bombardment in the Ghetto. According to Marek Edelman, the leader of the Bund fighting organization in the Ghetto, Henekh's vote broke a deadlock resulting in the decision to create the Jewish Combat Organization (the Bund's military group) in the Warsaw Ghetto. Henekh and his wife were captured and sent to the Majdanek death camp near Lublin for four months. I read that he had engaged in acts of heroism while incarcerated. He and his wife were ultimately sent to *Werk Tze,* the section of the notorious munitions factory commandeered by the Germans in the town of Skarzysko-Kamienna midway between Krakow and Warsaw. This factory had three sections, the third, *Werk Tse*, a combination factory and concentration camp, was reserved for Jews. The work in this part of the factory was so dangerous and toxic (they used picric acid as part of the munitions processing that literally turned the skin yellow) that the life expectancy of Jews in this setting was 3 months.

And I knew two more things. I knew that my uncle and his wife, along with others, were shot in the forest outside this camp in a failed attempt to escape following a rumor that the camp would be liquidated the following day. And I knew from the time I was a small boy that my father had always said: "If I knew where my brother Henekh was buried, I would bring flowers to his grave every day." These were words I never forgot, words that expressed both a connection and a loss too intense to comprehend. I had always imagined a "grave" waiting for flowers that would never come.

Mixed feelings regarding our trip to Poland gave way to clarity of purpose. I did not know where or how my family perished. Only Henekh's journey could be traced, and, with the help of my research efforts, Internet, and modern technology, I was intent on addressing my father's wish. I found a map of the factory where my uncle and aunt had been incarcerated in Felicia Karay's book about the Skarzysko camp, Death Comes in Yellow. With the help of Google Earth, I was able to superimpose that map on the current map of Skarzysko. I contacted the local historical

53

museum in the town and was informed that parts of the factory still exist, that it is still a munitions plant, but that it makes classified weapons (many of which, ironically, it sells to Israel), and that I would need permission to visit. My goals were to visit the ruins of *Werk Tse* if they were to be found and the forest where my uncle was murdered. With this information in hand, I was able to surmise the approximate location of where *Werk Tse* stood and that a forest still exists outside the factory complex. As expected, it was to the east, precisely the direction they would have gone in 1944 to reach the advancing Soviet army. With help from the local museum staff, I was able to contact the factory administrator and set a date for a visit for my wife, my children and me. We arranged to have a guide as well who would drive us from Krakow to Skarzysko and on to Warsaw, our final destination. My plan was simple; lay flowers at the ruins of *Werk Tse*.

In Krakow, we stayed in what had been the Jewish quarter, on the block lined with "Jewish" restaurants, each with its own ensemble playing Yiddish folks tunes and klezmer music into the night. Initially odd and off-putting, there was an air of respectfulness among the locals we met, and, for me, a kind of strange familiarity that counterbalanced an otherwise bizarre and awkward scene. We visited Auschwitz and toured Krakow, including the site where the Krakow Ghetto had stood. On July 30th, coincident with the exact day that my uncle and aunt were killed (this was not planned), we bought a bouquet of flowers, and were off to do what we set out to do. That very morning, however, I received an email from an administrator at the munitions factory stating that he regretted to inform me that the factory was about to start its annual two week summer holiday and that our visit could not take place. I asked our guide for advice. He said we should not respond, check in with the museum staff first, and then make our way to the factory and "play dumb." If asked, I was to lie about getting the email that morning. This made me very anxious (I am not a good liar), but fittingly seemed to evoke the uncertainty and tension of an earlier time. We followed his instructions. The museum staff could not have been friendlier or more welcoming, and, in a show of support and enthusiasm, two of them piled into our van in a scene reminiscent of *"Little Miss Sunshine,"* and we were off to the factory. Our guide took the lead, spoke with Security, and after what seemed like an eternity, arranged an impromptu meeting with a plant administrator. A long and tense discussion took place in Polish in the parking lot of a surviving factory building. I was not called upon to lie, but did learn during the negotiations that *Werk Tse* no longer stood. However, there was a memorial at the site of *Werk Tse*, which they referred to as the *"Patelnye,"* which was absolutely off limits for a visit. The word *"patelnye"* was instantly recognizable to me as it was one of the many Polish words that made its way into Yiddish vernacular and my family's kitchen. It is the word for frying pan, and came to epitomize the horrifying conditions of the labor camp in the most grotesque terms imaginable. I also learned that the larger factory complex had its own memorial. It was located in the surviving and refurbished building immediately in front of us. They called it the Room of Remembrance and it was dedicated to all those who had perished in the era, Poles, and Jews alike. After what seemed like endless negotiations, we were informed, begrudgingly, that the administrator could take me alone into that room, and just for a minute. Realizing this was the best I could do, I took my flowers and followed her to the room. Among the various military artifacts and other memorabilia in the room was a simple stone memorial dedicated to the Jews who had perished. In an experience that was robbed of meaning and emotion, I lay the flowers down in a perfunctory manner, and left.

But my real goal, to honor my father's wish to visit my uncle's "grave," was not yet realized. Naturally, there was no grave, but there was the expanse of forest immediately adjacent to the site where the camp had stood. I knew that somewhere in that forest, my uncle, aunt, and others had been shot. After dropping our new friends at the museum, I instructed our guide to drive down the road that bordered the forest. At a small dirt road, which I found on Google Earth, I asked him to stop. My wife, daughter, son, and I walked down the road to a small clearing in the forest.

This was certainly not the spot where Henekh perished, but it would have to do. We read my uncle's biography. My son chanted *El Malei Rachamim*, the memorial prayer for the dead. We hugged and shed some tears. I suddenly felt this pang in my heart; I had used the flowers to support our ill-fated visit to the factory, and could therefore not fulfill my father's wish to lay flowers on Henekh's "grave." And just as suddenly, I had this epiphany. I had, in fact, fulfilled his wish. My children and my family were his flowers. We had done what we set out to do.

But the story does not end there. There is a postscript. Part of our itinerary in Warsaw included a visit to the museum, *POLIN*, dedicated to the thousand-year history of Jews in Poland. It is a magical place, first rate, detailed, comprehensive, and beautiful. After wandering through centuries in the galleries, we walk into a gallery devoted to the history of Jewish political movements between the two World Wars. We approach the section devoted to the Jewish Labor Bund. The exhibit includes several "Ken Burns style" slide shows depicting photographs of the era. As I watched one of these slide shows I gazed upon a photograph of a large group of young people in boats on a lake. To the right in the photograph was a handsome man, bare-chested, wearing sunglasses. I swear it is my father. But I am very familiar with how the unconscious desire to see things can influence what you see. I call my wife and ask her, without preparation or warning, to watch the slide show. "Oh my G-d, it's your father!" I break down. She then goes to a second slide show in the exhibit. She says, "Quick, come here. It's a picture of Henekh." He is marching in a parade, his clear and piercing eyes evident, dressed in the uniform of his party. The poignancy of the moment does not escape me. For however long this museum will stand, my father and his beloved brother will be together. And, perhaps for at least a brief moment in time, one brother's wish will have been honored, bringing a modicum of peace to another brother's soul.

The Doppler Effect

The D train doors closed just as Sammy stepped onto the platform of the West 4th Street station. Slightly miffed, he was nevertheless glad to be out of the January cold. He removed his pipe from the pocket of his overcoat, filled the bowl with loose tobacco, tamped it down into a wad, and lit it with a strike anywhere match he ran across the metal No Smoking sign on the station wall.

"When's the next train?" Sammy asked a transit cop standing near the end of the platform.

"There's no smoking in the subway, sonny."

Sammy, twenty-six, leaned back and sized up the cop through squinted eyes peering out from under his Stetson fedora. As he did so, he shifted the pipe bit from one corner of his mouth to the other, the black-dyed peach fuzz

Originally published in *Literally Stories*, July 5, 2023

on his upper lip in full view. He exhaled a puff of smoke.

"Sorry, officer. I thought it meant cigarettes."

Sammy flashed a disdainful smile and pivoted on his heel. He took several steps on the yellow warning line, arms extended from his sides, pretending to be a tightrope walker. After a fake stumble, he calmly regained his balance. Using his free hand, he knocked the glowing clump of tobacco from his pipe onto the tracks and turned again toward the cop.

The transit cop pointed toward a sign suspended from the station ceiling some thirty yards behind Sammy.

"Read the electronic board. Twelve minutes. And stay off the damn yellow line, asshole."

The transit cop performed a pivot of his own, not nearly as practiced as Sammy's, and positioned himself against the white tile wall at the end of the platform.

•

Sammy's ability to dodge the cop's chiding was honed by years of dodging his mother's. He was a pro at deception and sleight of hand.

"Sammy, why don't you eat? Eat a little more ... for me," his mother would beg him, the pleas beginning when he was eight or nine. "You're skin and bones!"

Unperturbed, he responded, "I am eating, Mom. Look," pointing to his empty plate which he had cleverly cleared while his mother wasn't looking.

Sammy's glib attitude toward eating belied the seriousness of his condition. He suffered from a severe case of anorexia nervosa. After years of therapy beginning when he was ten, frequent medical and psychiatric hospitalizations and two near-death experiences because of electrolyte imbalances, the best Sammy could do was teeter on the brink of malnutrition.

When he entered his twenties, he thought of himself as a man trapped in a boy's body. Sammy wore thick-soled shoes to make his five-foot frame look taller. He hovered around eighty pounds. Because he never made it to a normal weight during adolescence, Sammy missed puberty.

"Doc, I've never been able to jerk off," Sammy informed his pediatrician when he was sixteen.

"Have you ever had a wet dream?" the doctor inquired.

"Not that I can remember."

"You would remember."

The doctor ordered a battery of hormone tests. The news was not good. He would remain prepubertal forever.

Learning that he would never be able to perform sexually in the way he had hoped was upsetting to Sammy, but he kept his feelings to himself.

Still, he had dreams—dry ones, that is—and ambitions.

"I am going to be a magician," Sammy declared to his parents when he was eleven. He read every available magic book in the Kew Gardens library. He took a job stocking shelves in the neighborhood C Town Supermarket as soon as he was old enough to work so he could buy Marvin's Amazing Magic Tricks and a host of other magic kits for kids.

"Another magic kit? Better you should study your geometry. Make something of yourself," Sammy's father scolded.

"I love magic. And I'm good at it too," Sammy countered. Sammy was a decent student but his father was right; his heart wasn't in geometry.

During his mid-teens, he performed his act at every neighborhood birthday party that would have him. One thing led to another, and he soon became a regular on the local bar mitzvah and magic club circuits. He called himself Sammy the Sorcerer.

He lived in his late grandmother's rent stabilized studio apartment on the Lower East Side. With help from his parents, disability checks, and the occasional gig, he was beginning to make a life for himself.

•

Sammy had twelve minutes to kill until the next D train was scheduled to arrive. Leaving the cop behind, he proceeded to the opposite end of the platform where the last subway car would stop. By boarding the car closest to the exit he needed at the 42nd Steet station, he figured he'd save himself a minute or two. He was headed to Houdini's Haunt, a new magic shop on 44th near Bryant

Park. Except for the transit cop who had parked himself at the opposite end of the station, the platform seemed empty, unusual for a Saturday at nine a.m.

Sammy then caught a glimpse of a young woman standing nearby. She appeared to be about his age. Her short, spiked hair, eye shadow and eye liner, lipstick, leather jacket, extremely short leather skirt, wide-hole fishnet tights and Doc Martens were all black. She was carrying a small black handbag as well, its thin strap draped across her chest.

The woman was precariously leaning over the tracks, her left foot on the yellow marker and her right foot securely planted several feet back at a forty-five-degree angle. She was looking up the tunnel for a sign of the next train. Sammy was accustomed to observing fellow New Yorkers engage in this risky ritual presumably intended to magically make the train come faster.

"You shouldn't lean out like that," Sammy remarked, hoping the woman had not seen his antics at the other end of the station.

The woman stepped back from the edge of the platform but did not acknowledge him. Her eyes were focused on the smooth concrete beneath her feet.

Arms folded, she began to pace along a path parallel to the subway tracks and at a safe distance from the yellow stripe. This back-and-forth motion persisted for about a minute or two. Sammy watched intently.

Although her goth appearance was somewhat off-putting to Sammy, he could see that she was quite beautiful. Her light blue eyes and pale complexion sharply contrasted with her black hair and clothing. His eyes were drawn to her leather skirt, which he thought was far too short for winter but suited her shapely body. As she walked, her skirt rose and fell. He could see a row of cuts on her upper thigh through the holes in the fishnet tights. The cut furthest down on her thigh was oozing blood.

"Are you okay?" Sammy tried again.

The woman did not respond. The trajectory of her pacing grew more elliptical, approaching the platform edge with each orbit, and her stride quickened.

"Yo!" Sammy raised his voice. He glanced at the digital sign. The train was just five minutes from the station. The woman did not respond. Desperate to get the woman's attention, he blurted out the first thing he could think to say.

"Hey ... have you ever heard of the Doppler effect?" Sammy immediately felt stupid asking such a random question.

To his astonishment, the woman stopped pacing and took two deliberate steps toward him, her arms still folded, a quizzical look on her face.

"What did you say?"

"The Doppler effect," Sammy repeated more emphatically. "You can hear it when subway trains come and go.

The pitch gets higher as they approach and reaches a crescendo as they pull into the station. Then the pitch gets lower as the trains speed away." He took a breath.

"Why the hell are you telling me this?" the woman asked, her stare piercing Sammy.

"I don't want you to jump." Sammy insisted.

The woman glared at him.

"Whatever you are feeling now will pass. I'm sure of it." His voice grew more tender.

"Well, fuck you. Get out of my way!"

"Well," Sammy echoed, "for your information, I'm killing myself too. The difference is I am doing it slowly." Sammy shocked himself with his disclosure.

His revelation had no impact. The woman resumed her elliptical pacing but more frantic than before.

Sammy suddenly stepped in front of her and raised two fists near her face. He opened both hands, palms out, revealing there was nothing inside. Stunned by this maneuver, the woman stopped.

He then made a fist with his right hand and slowly began pulling a red silk scarf from it with his left. "Voila!"

"What the hell?" The sound of the train could be heard in the distance. The woman stepped to the left, her own fists clenched. Sammy mirrored her movement and prevented her from getting around him.

As he did so, he dropped the red scarf on the ground and pulled out a rainbow-colored scarf, this time from his left fist. "Presto!"

"Get out of my way you creep!" The train would soon be upon them, judging from the sound emerging from the tunnel.

Sammy did not relent. He reached behind the woman's right ear and produced a carnation. The sound of the train reached a fever pitch as it entered the station.

The woman screamed as loudly as she possibly could, but no one other than Sammy was there to hear her. He stood several feet from the woman, between her and the arriving train. The sound of her screams and the screeching of the brakes hurt his ears, but he did not move.

As the train slowed, her folded arms fell to her sides, her shoulders sank and her clenched fists relaxed. The woman's screaming gave way to crying. Her face softened and her tears fell to the platform.

Full stop ... pause ... hiss. The subway doors opened. Several passengers emerged.

Sammy and the woman stood there looking at each other. He wanted to ask if she felt better, but dared not.

The sternness in the woman's face was gone. She tried to wipe her tears with the back of her hands, but only managed to smudge her cheeks. She then reached toward Sammy's hand and took the carnation.

"Can I call someone for you?"

The woman shook her head. "Thank you. I'll be alright. I know what to do."

Sammy heard the subway doors close behind him. Now it was Sammy who looked down at the concrete platform. The only sound in the station was the shuffling feet of departing passengers headed for the exits.

"Can I call you ... you know ... to make sure you're alright?" Sammy was barely able to get the words out.

The woman opened her handbag, took out a pen and scribbled her phone number on the back of a theater ticket stub.

"Astrid." She handed Sammy her phone number as the train lurched forward. "You missed your train."

"Sammy. No worries. I can catch the next one."

The Ghost of Kyiv

Pavel shot up from his knees, barely having time to make the sign of the cross, when he heard the cruise missile strike his motherland.

"To hell with you!" Pavel raised his clenched fists in the air, then brought them down quickly.

The missile strike interrupted the evening prayers at St. Sophia Cathedral where Pavel regularly attended. Services at the church, a religious landmark in Kyiv, were now being held outside to ensure the safety of the faithful. The other parishioners, unlike Pavel, ducked and covered when they heard the unmistakable sound of the rocket overhead. After a brief silence, they slowly got to their feet.

"Another one, devil take it," grunted the gnarled, blue-eyed grandmother, her dislodged kerchief revealing a full

Originally published in *Of TheBook, September 2024*

head of white hair. She brushed herself off and glanced furtively at the priest, hoping he did not hear her blasphemy. Just in case, she whispered a prayer of reparation sotto voce.

"Where there is one, there usually are more...like vermin," commented the church custodian while continuing to survey the skies.

Although everyone in attendance braced themselves for additional strikes, none came. "Where do you suppose the missile landed?" the custodian continued, talking to no one in particular.

"Looks like it could be somewhere near the park." Pavel saw smoke rise to the northwest.

Pavel was a patriot of Ukraine, who, like his fellow countrymen, detested the Russian despot. Like most of his brethren, he decided to stand his ground against the anticipated massive Russian assault. He had spent three years in the Ukrainian army reserves and was comfortable around weaponry and munitions, urban tactics, and hand-to-hand combat. Pavel was stoutly built, biceps and quads thickened by years of high-rise construction work. Not a stickler for protocol, he wore his military garb informally, shirt collar open, a blue beret with yellow tassel on his head. Since the time the Russian troops massed on Ukraine's northern borders, he carried his AK-47 wherever he went. Pavel could easily have been mistaken for a partisan from an earlier era.

The small crowd outside St. Sophia's slowly dispersed. Pavel lingered and found himself alone except for the alcoholic amputee who permanently made his home and his living in the outer vestibule of the cathedral. The two briefly exchanged glances after which Pavel slipped away and hurried the six blocks to his studio apartment.

Pavel, a man in his early forties, lived alone. There had been some women, but he always stopped short of a proposal of marriage when one was likely called for. He did not mind solitude and was completely self-reliant. Safe in his apartment, he positioned his weapon next to the door and removed his fatigues, haphazardly placing them on a chair. He took a shot of his favorite Polish vodka, as was his custom, and settled into bed under a goose-down quilt. Images of the missile strike returned as he slept but did not awaken him.

The next morning, Pavel awoke earlier than usual and decided to explore the site of destruction from the previous evening. In contrast to the typical early-morning bustle of the Kyiv streets before the Russian invasion, stores were closed for the most part, mothers were not hurrying children off to school, and the buses and trolleys were not running.

Dogs, however, were barking. "The first line of defense against the Russian onslaught," Pavel mused.

Pavel was content to hike the eight kilometers to where he thought the ruins would be; he had no patrol assignment that day, and the brisk winter air was invigorating. He reached the site after an hour and fifteen minutes and was shocked by what he saw. There were several soldiers and emergency responders searching through the rubble of the memorial park that was Babi Yar.

"I saw the missile land last night from St. Sophia's. What's the damage?" Pavel asked a worker, a search dog obediently at his side.

"Five dead. Searched through the night, but I think that's all of them. No one alive that we can find," the emergency worker with the dog responded, looking exhausted from the night's work. "They must have been out for a stroll or something."

"Of all places to bomb," Pavel remarked angrily, nodding in the direction of one of the memorials.

"We think they were aiming for the TV tower but hit the burial site instead. Russian marksmanship." The emergency worker turned and spat on the ground in the direction of the tower.

Pavel was two generations removed from the horror of Babi Yar, but he knew the story well. As a boy he had only heard rumors of the atrocities that had occurred in the ravines, now covered by grass and shrubs. Neither his parents nor his grandparents had wanted to talk about it. And certainly, neither did the Soviets. The Soviets did all they could to cover it up, first with mud, then with a sports stadium. Neither plan came to fruition. The desecration that was the hideous TV tower, however, relentlessly bathing the landscape with microwaves, could not be avoided.

Pavel ambled further into the park and came upon the Babi Yar synagogue, a structure completed the previous year to commemorate the massacres. It was a curious building, made mostly of wood, looking like a big tome when closed, and opening like a child's pop-up book. The synagogue unfolded into a three-dimensional space with all the required elements to facilitate prayer and contemplation. Pavel had taken notice of it as it was being built and admired its design. He approached the edifice to assess any damage. There was none. He noticed, however, the "book" that was the synagogue in its closed configuration was slightly ajar. He thought the blast might have caused the structure to shudder and crack open a bit.

Pavel, a devout Eastern Orthodox Christian, felt somewhat anxious to enter strange spiritual territory. His legs seemed heavier than before. He'd grown up among a few Jewish neighbors in Kyiv but had little to do with them. Still, he did not actively join in the undercurrent of antisemitism in his parochial school. In fact, he had occasion to defend a Jewish boy, a neighbor about his age who lived on his block.

"Get away from that Zionist antichrist or you'll get what's coming to him!"

"Piss off." Pavel was younger but much bigger than the two student hoodlums.

Although his defense of the boy cost him a bruised cheek and derision at the hands of his compatriots, Pavel felt confident he had done what he needed to do.

Pavel proceeded cautiously toward the open edge of the "book" and ever so gingerly pulled on one wall to better glimpse what was inside. As he did so, he noticed words that he recognized as Hebrew on the various parts of the wall, along with some beautiful iconography on a sky-blue background. The workmanship of the woodwork was first rate, each joint tight, but leaving just enough space for expansion. As he pulled further on the wall, a part of the flooring emerged, then a pew, enough so that he could sit.

"How the world has turned upside down," Pavel said to himself, thinking he was completely alone. His thoughts turned to the irony of his current situation, a Christian alone in this synagogue built for Jews, the living next to the dead.

"Will someone build a church for us when all this is done?" he wondered, images of the ruins of his city and his country flooding his consciousness. "How many corpses will be added to those beneath me?" Thick clouds had gathered directly overhead. He noticed it was getting dark, although it was still the middle of the morning.

Pavel turned with a startle, reflexively pointing his rifle in the direction of the sound of rustling inside the synagogue. He was able to make out a figure, but just barely. It had grown so dark. He saw what appeared to be a boy, perhaps eleven or twelve years old, stumble slowly from the recesses of the structure.

"Who's there?" Pavel barked. "Come out, come out now, with your hands up in the air!"

The boy took a step forward, then another, unsteady, looking like a newborn fawn barely standing yet forced to walk. Pavel could begin to make out details. It was indeed a boy. He had a baby face, sunken cheeks, and his forehead was smudged with grime. He was wearing a longish coat that looked like it had belonged to an older brother, open in the front, baggy pants that appeared to be slipping from his waist, and a cap that was flat, like those worn by the boys who hustled in the streets. Pavel thought he could make out curly locks of hair wrapped around each ear under the hat, the kind he had seen on his Jewish neighbors. The boy appeared terrified, his smoky eyes wide and his hands trembling at his sides.

"I told you to put your hands up!" Pavel shouted while lowering his weapon, realizing there was no threat here, but insisting on obedience under such strange circumstances.

"What's your name?" Pavel's voice softened. "Where are you from? You look like you haven't eaten in days."

The boy did not appear to understand what Pavel was saying, so Pavel put down his weapon and motioned the boy to sit next to him. He took out a buttered roll, a pampushka, he had been saving for lunch and offered it to the boy. The boy cautiously took the roll in his hand, moved it close to his mouth, but then abruptly returned it to Pavel. He had a confused and sad look in his eyes, as though he did not remember how to eat.

When he returned the roll, the boy said: *"A sheynem dank...kh'bin nisht hungerik."*

Pavel did not have the slightest clue what the boy had said. He spoke in a language he did not understand but that he had overheard several times in the market, spoken by Hasidic tourists who were journeying to the grave of a famous rabbi. He thought it was Yiddish, at least that's what his Jewish neighbors had said the Hasidim were speaking. Pavel thought this might be the son of some such Hasid who got lost in the pandemonium, among the throngs of women and children rushing to escape Kyiv.

The boy, his body less tense, seemed to recognize too that he and this stranger were unable to communicate.

"Are you Jewish? Zhid?" The boy's face blanched and he took off to the shadows of the partially open synagogue.

Recognizing his inquiry terrified the boy, Pavel approached him with outstretched arms, his palms up, doing all he could to reassure him.

The boy re-emerged, reached into his coat, and pulled something out of his pocket which he handed to Pavel. It was a rolled cigarette, a bit tattered but dry. Although he did not smoke, Pavel took it and thanked him by repeatedly nodding.

Not sure what to do next, Pavel tried to work out how to reunite this lost boy with his family. He thought for a minute, asking himself what he could say so that the boy would not scamper off again.

"Mama?" Pavel asked the boy, exaggerating his mouth movements as if this would aid in the boy's comprehension. "Papa?"

The boy nodded, revealing he understood. The boy's affirmation, however, was followed by his shrinking further into his long coat and lowering his head so Pavel could only see the crown of his cap. Pavel decided he would take the boy to a shelter in Kyiv where he could be safe and get food. Perhaps there would be people there who could understand him and help reunite the boy with his family.

Pavel gently grasped the boy's hand and took a step in the direction of town to indicate he should come with him. "Mama? Papa?"

Just then, a MiG-29 soared just over their heads. The noise was deafening. Pavel, distracted, excitedly shouted to himself, "It's the Ghost of Kyiv! He's one of ours! He'll teach those sons of bitches a thing or two!"

Pavel did not notice the boy slip his hand from his grip. By the time the jet disappeared over the horizon Pavel realized the boy had drifted toward the ravine. Some five meters away, he noticed for the first time a large red stain surrounding a kopiyka size round hole in the back of the boy's flat cap.

Unable to follow, Pavel watched as the image of his diminutive companion faded into the darkness of the day, over a knoll, and into a ravine that seemed to swallow him whole.

Pavel sat stunned, possessed by the boy. Far off voices from the remaining workers near the tower eased into his consciousness. Glancing over his shoulder to where the missile took the lives of five innocents, Pavel's stupor slowly turned to wakefulness. His wakefulness swelled to rage and determination. Pavel clutched his AK-47 tightly, put the cigarette the boy had given him in the corner of his mouth, adjusted his beret, and marched off to face the tanks with the Z insignias.

Broken Glass

"*Mazl tov! Mazl tov.* We should only meet for celebrations! May God bless you and your betrothed with good health and happiness all the days of your lives! *L'chaim!*"

The man's unkempt beard caught a few drops of Glenfiddich as he lowered the shot glass from his mouth and slammed it emphatically on the table. His beard, like those of the dozens of other black-hatted guests, added ten years to his appearance.

"Thank you, Reb Motl," the groom's father, Avram, responded to the man with whom he had just shared his third *l'chaim*. A smile was plastered on Avram's face. "And soon the same by you!"

Dovid, the groom, sat between his father and his

Originally published in Fig Tree Lit, 2024

father-in-law-to-be at the head of the *tish*, the table, at the event also termed a *tish*—the men's-only gathering before the wedding ceremony. Avram privately turned to his son. His smile was gone. "Did you take your medication?"

"Not today, Tatti. I fasted since morning. I'm not drinking."

Avram's elastic smile snapped back into place, but he could not stop his brow from furrowing.

The congratulatory ritual was repeated dozens of times, albeit with Avram lifting an empty shot glass after his fifth *l'chaim*. Dovid's father-in-law-to-be, Itzik, flanking Dovid at the table, stopped after six. The local rabbinic dignitaries from the Lakewood, New Jersey area, relatives from as far away as Detroit, fellow congregants, business associates, and even the occasional interloper working the crowd for charitable contributions offered their best wishes to the troika. Dovid attempted to show off his scholarly prowess by lecturing to the assembled, but was good-naturedly heckled, consistent with tradition. In short order, Dovid would be escorted by the fathers from the tish down a hall to a room where the *badekn*, the veiling of the bride, would take place.

Without gesture or pronouncement, lines of yeshiva students with interlocked arms, all Dovid's friends, faced the threesome and began walking backwards. The students pulled them along as if with divine magnetic attraction. A makeshift phalanx of men marched behind and nudged the trio forward; there was no turning back. As all parties fell into place, the frenzied sound of *badekn* music rose from the male chorus with riotous clapping and brass accompaniment.

The bride, Hannah, sat motionless on her throne next to the mothers and the female entourage, her face beaming. The women waited for the moment Dovid would greet his bride and place the opaque veil upon her face. The distant sound of singing grew louder. Young boys, like scouts approaching Canaan, excitedly ran ahead to the women, signaling the arrival of the main column.

The groom-embedded trio approached the bride and the throng of female guests. Itzik lovingly placed his hands on the sides of his daughter's head, repeating the blessing he had bestowed on her every Sabbath since her birth. Avram did the same for his son. The mothers wept on cue.

Now it was Dovid's turn. He moved forward looking directly into the bride's face. They had not seen each other for days.

"This is not Hannah," Dovid said in a voice that could not be heard above the din of the crowd. He looked away. "This is not Hannah!" he repeated more loudly. Now his voice rose above the assembly.

Hannah's enraptured expression morphed to quizzical, then horrified. The attendees appeared stunned, and the singing stopped. Hundreds of pairs of eyes struggled to avoid each other.

Avram grabbed his son by the arm and rushed him into an adjoining room, escorted by a rising cacophony of disbelief.

"What is this?" Avram yelled through his clenched jaw. He squeezed Dovid's arms tightly.

Dovid said nothing. Avram shook him to force a response.

His son stared through his father's contorted face.

"It's not Hannah. Can't you see?" Dovid's voice was weak and desperate.

"Dovid." Avram's eyes glazed over, and his tone softened. "It's a dybbuk. He's back. The same you battled in the hospital last year. Don't you remember?"

Dovid was already gone. His body slumped onto a nearby chair. He sat with his eyes closed, no longer a part of this world.

•

Dovid awoke in the Emergency Room of Monmouth Medical Center, the closest hospital with a psychiatry service. An IV had been inserted into his arm, delivering the Ativan that was helping him manage the catatonic state in which he found himself. He had been here before.

"Tell me, Dovid, do you know where you are?" asked a young woman in a white coat standing before him.

Dovid, though only able to move his head a few degrees, took in the IV pole with its attendant pump, the bed with siderails, and the blood pressure machine. Then he looked back at the woman with a large Monmouth ID clipped to the breast pocket of that long white coat. The initials "M.D." appeared after her name.

"I think I'm in a hospital," Dovid answered after a long pause.

"Yes. You're at Monmouth. And do you know today's date?"

Dovid's eyes shut with force, the pain in his brain showing through. Another pause.

"I was supposed to get married today."

"That's what I heard. What happened?" the doctor asked.

"They tricked me. I was supposed to marry Hannah, but it was someone else sitting in her chair. Just like Leah and Rachel."

The doctor's puzzled expression revealed she did not understand the biblical reference. Genesis relates the story of Jacob, the Jewish patriarch, believing he was marrying his true love, Rachel, only to discover after the wedding that it had been Leah, the older sister, under the veil.

"Who tricked you? Who was the woman in the bride's chair?"

"As if you don't know," Dovid answered, turning away from the doctor.

"Honestly, I don't. Who?"

"I have no idea who arranged for a strange woman to take Hannah's place. If you don't know, why don't you ask the people who were there?"

"You mean your father? He arrived with you in the ambulance."

"My father is dead. I don't know who you are talking about."

The doctor excused herself and searched for Dovid's father to obtain further history.

"They said he might be suffering from schizophrenia when he was hospitalized last year. Before he was hospitalized then, Dovid began to act in strange ways. He started davening...praying, night and day, without stopping to eat, without bathing, and without sleeping. It was like he was possessed. We went to our rabbi for advice, and he told us to take him here, to the emergency room. Then he went upstairs to the...unit...you know..."

"The Behavioral Health Unit?"

"Yes. That one. But we transferred him after a few days to a hospital outside our area that specialized in Orthodox Jewish patients.

"And they said he might have schizophrenia?" asked the doctor. "Was he showing other symptoms?"

"He became mistrustful of everyone. He said he could hear the voice of *Hashem*, God, just like you talking to me. He saw dead relatives in the dark, and he spoke to them. He said they spoke back. We were terrified."

"Because of the seriousness of his illness?"

"Yes, of course. But also because of what it means in

our community. Who would marry such a man?"

"I see. Did they start him on medication?"

"Yes. Risperione, Risdal...something like that."

"Risperidone?"

"Yes. That's it. Dovid didn't like it. Made him drowsy, lightheaded. But it helped."

"How so?"

"In three weeks, we had our son back. He seemed back to normal. It was a *nes*...a miracle."

•

"He's such a fucking loser."

"No shit. Have you seen the shnoz on that guy?"

"And stuuupid? No one wanted to be his study partner!"

"And...he smells. Quickest way to clear the *beys medresh* during study hall is to have him walk in!"

"That's a good one!"

"That's what happens when you play with yourself all day."

Dovid opened his eyes and looked around the sparingly furnished room. The desk, chair, and end table next to his bed were all bolted to the floor. He could make out the curtains, attached by Velcro loops to a flimsy curtain rod that could barely support the fabric, let alone a body. He took this all in and remembered he had been here before.

"Hey shmuck. Why don't you just kill yourself?"

The voices in Dovid's head would not stop.

"Who are you?" Dovid demanded, the question slipping from his lips at a barely audible volume.

No answer.

Dovid's tone grew angry. "What kind of dybbuks are you? Stop lying about me!"

"Oh, no, he doesn't like us. That makes me sad," one voice said.

Dovid flew into a rage. "Get the fuck out of here, you assholes!"

"Did you ever hear such language?"

The door to Dovid's room flew open.

"Are you alright?" The psych tech did not wait for an answer. "Who are you screaming at, man?"

Dovid turned to the Black attendant with the Jamaican accent and saw his eyes were kind. Dovid lowered a fist that he had not even been aware of and slunk down onto the edge of the bed.

"No one." Dovid was glad for the intrusion of a real human being, but he was not ready to engage. He lay down and turned his body toward the wall.

"I'm just outside if you need me."

Dovid said no more.

•

"Crab grass syndrome?" Avram repeated what he thought he heard Dovid's doctor say.

"No. Capgras Syndrome. It's when someone believes family, friends, anyone, are not really who they are. People with Capgras Syndrome are convinced they are surrounded by imposters. It can occur in a variety of serious psychiatric illnesses, including schizophrenia."

Avram listened intently to every word the doctor said. His brain, more accustomed to unraveling Talmudic conundrums, tried hard to digest this information, the effort reflected in a tic of the left eye that emerged only under stress.

"He didn't have this the first time around." Avram's tone conveyed the injustice of this additional burden.

"It happens. We don't know why," the doctor countered.

"So that's why he didn't recognize Hannah?"

"Presumably."

"Will he get better?"

"He should respond to the medication he was taking…" The doctor interrupted himself. "The medicine he was supposed to be taking."

"He told me he missed one dose. On the day of the wedding."

"That's highly unlikely," the doctor interjected. "More likely he stopped the Risperidone weeks or even months before. I will talk with Dovid about considering an injectable form of the medication that he can get at a doctor's office every month. That may be easier, and more dependable."

"Thank you, Doctor. Please make my Dovidl better."

•

"I would like to see Dovid Einhorn. He was admitted here last week. Eleven North."

The woman at the reception desk did not look up. "And you are?"

"Hannah Cohen. His fiancée."

"Has Mr. Einhorn agreed to see you?" the reception-ist asked, though she knew the answer. The only visitors Dovid Einhorn had put on his approved visitation list were his parents. HIPAA regulations prohibited the staff at the Behavioral Health Unit of Monmouth Medical Center from even confirming a given individual was a patient in the hospital without authorization.

"He isn't expecting me," Hannah acknowledged. "But I'm sure he'll see me. Please." There was a hint of desper-ation in her voice.

The receptionist finally looked up. Hannah could see the woman was wearing a *shaytl*, a wig worn by married women in the Orthodox Lakewood community. Her expres-sion suggested she knew the whole story. Lakewood, after all, is a shtetl. No secrets.

"Let me see what I can do." There was a drop of pity in her voice, as if she could imagine for an excruciating moment what it must have felt like to be stood up at the *khupe.* "Please take a seat in the lobby. I'll come get you."

The receptionist called the unit and asked the nurse to ask Dovid if he'd agree to see Hannah Cohen. He did. The receptionist, only four foot ten and wearing a long-sleeved blouse buttoned at the neck, a skirt down to her ankles, and white sneakers, retrieved Hannah from the lobby. "Take this elevator to the eleventh floor and follow the signs for Eleven North," she said, pointing to the elevator bank to her right. "The door will be locked. Ring the doorbell and a staff member will let you in."

•

"Hello Dovid. How are you feeling?"

"Hannah...I was expecting Hannah..."

"I am Hannah, Dovid. Don't you remember?"

Dovid bolted down the corridor, away from her, his *tsitsit* flying behind him. "I don't know who you are." He stopped and turned back to face her. "What have you done with Hannah?" he demanded.

One week into the hospitalization, Dovid's voices were quieter. The degradation he had experienced at the hands of the two evil commentators had been silenced by the antipsychotic medication. But he was still far from well.

Hannah stood her ground. "I am Hannah, Dovid. Your Hannah. And I'm not going anywhere."

Dovid pivoted, marched into his room, and slammed the door.

Hannah did all she could to make it off the unit before bursting into tears.

She returned the very next day, confidently claiming she was on the approved list of visitors. This was not inaccurate. After all, it was Dovid who was in error, not Hannah.

"Oh, you're back. What is your name, anyway"?

Hannah knew better than to provoke Dovid again.

"Rachel."

"Are you making fun of me? I am Dovid, not Jacob."

Hannah resisted the temptation to say, "I am Hannah, your Rachel," but thought better of it.

"No...I am Rachel...really." She sat on a coffee-stained armchair with frayed upholstery opposite him and stared at the worn carpet between them.

"Well, believe me when I say that switching Hannah for you was no less cruel than switching Leah for Rachel."

"I can understand that. It must have been quite a shock."

Dovid did not anticipate someone, let alone this strange woman, taking his side. "Yes. Yes, it was an extreme shock. I just want to know what happened to her."

"You are worried."

"Yes."

"You loved her very much."

"I love her very much." Dovid began to cry.

"I can see that."

A patient entered the day room and sat down on the couch in front of the television. He reached for the remote control and turned it on. The volume had been left at a near-maximum setting.

"I'd better get going."

"Will you come back to see me...Rachel?"

"I will. Tomorrow."

•

And so, it went, day after day. Hannah's relentless compassion coupled with the blockade of dopamine receptors in Dovid's brain worked together to bring him back from madness. The breakthrough came on the eighteenth day. The couple met in the empty day room as had become their custom.

"Good to see you, Hannah. I knew you would come."

"You recognize me?"

"I may be crazy, but I'm not dumb. Of course, I recognize you. Good to see you after such a long time. You came to say good-bye."

Hannah's body stiffened. "Why good-bye?"

"Of course, good-bye. I sinned. At your expense."

"What sin?"

"I humiliated you, in front of your family, your friends, our friends. I tripped us both on the way to the *khupe*."

"You didn't sin. You were sick." Hannah began to walk around Dovid.

"Nevertheless. It doesn't matter. I am damaged."

"I love you, Dovid." Her circling continued.

"I am broken!" Dovid's voice grew loud but trembled at the same time. "The community will shun us. Children will laugh at our children. They'll mercilessly be teased. Or worse, they could carry the genes of a *meshugene!*"

"*Hashem* will help."

Dovid, fearful he would add blasphemy to his pile of troubles, did not respond.

"For us the glass is broken before the *khupe.*"

"We will join the pieces together."

"We will bleed."

"The mingling of our blood will strengthen us." Hannah stopped before Dovid, having completed exactly seven rotations.

"Then it is in the hands of *Hashem*. We are in the hands of *Hashem*."

Hannah and Dovid moved nearer to each other. Their faces were so close only a single ray of light from the secured window could pass between them.

The Baba

The *Baba*, as she was called, was not my *Baba*, nor was she my *bube* nor my *bobe*. I must have first set eyes on her when I was two and a half on a frigid February day, my first in Philadelphia, having been carried in tow by my parents from Cuba, my birthplace, along with my older sister. I don't remember the *Baba* at that first meeting, but the image of her that grew in my mind in the ensuing years was indelible. Short, wiry, sporting a stern, weathered face, and piercing green eyes, her gray hair in a bun, she was a force to be reckoned with. A look from her was enough.

Like I said, she was not my *Baba*. She belonged to my six-year-old cousin, or better put, he belonged to her. She watched over him intently, such that no evil, and, no evil

Originally published in The Jewish Writing Project, April 2023.

eye, should befall him. *Pu pu pu!* As doting as she was to him, that's how nasty she was to me. Why? What had I done to deserve such treatment? For him, she tolerated his fondling her soft dangling earlobes with his fingers. For me, a cold stare. The *Baba*, doubtless, regarded me as an intruder. Truth be told, my entire family was the intruder. The four of us moved into my aunt and uncle's already crowded row house for several months until my father could find work and we could rent a house of our own. Doubling and tripling up in bedrooms, competing for the single bathroom, and accommodating Cuban cuisine, were only some of the tensions. For the *Baba*, I became the focus of her displeasure.

The *Baba*, I later learned, actually had a name. *Khave.* She was the youngest of nineteen children, and the only person of that generation that I had encountered in my early life. I had assumed all in her generation, the generation of grandparents, had died before the war or were murdered in the calamity. The *Baba*, in sharp contrast to my parents, was tied to traditions against which many in my parents' generation rebelled. She lit candles on Shabbos, wearing a delicate white lace on her head when she did so, and recited the *brokhe* in an undertone. Unlike my parents, aunt and uncle who were "modern" Jews despite their Eastern European roots, she was a relic from the old country.

She also happened to be a terrific cook and literally

made everything from scratch. No dish more so than the *gefilte* fish she prepared for *peysakh*. I learned this in dramatic fashion when I wandered into the bathroom of my aunt's house and saw several very large fish swimming in the bathtub. They moved in the tub, ever so slightly, suggesting they were not dead, yet. I was startled, a bit disgusted, but asked no questions. I imagined the fish ended up in *Baba*'s kitchen but did not dwell on the thought. And I certainly never dared poke my head into the *Baba*'s command center. Entrance was strictly forbidden, lest I risk meeting the same fate as the fish.

As may seem obvious by now, I found life with the *Baba* frightening. Her demeanor toward me was unkind. She was harsh and uncaring. In one instance, she barred me from riding my cousin's tricycle, even though he was at school. Of course, I was a bit of an *antikl* (a rare piece of work, a "pistol") myself. Once, when she proclaimed I was not permitted to sit on the sofa in the living room for fear I might soil it, I decided to pee on it out of spite. To finish the story, my father, in what I still regard as among the greatest acts of kindness I have been blessed to receive, bought me my own tricycle with his very first paycheck.

These early years in Philadelphia were difficult for my family and I recall them as being somewhat dark. But *peysakh*, and the seders we shared with my aunt and uncle, my cousins, and yes, the *Baba*, were bright spots of those years. The *Baba* would start things off with candle lighting.

My father and uncle, both lifelong Bundists, Jewish socialists who abandoned religion in favor of a Yiddish cultural
milieu, took turns chanting from the Haggadah in fluent
Hebrew at lightning speed. They had attended *kheyder* in
Poland as boys, and the words and tropes returned each
year as reliably as monarch butterflies. The effect was hypnotic, albeit strange and out of character. They stopped
reading when they got tired, or when the rest of us
clamored that it was time to eat. Whatever commentary
accompanied the seder was in Yiddish, the lingua franca
of our families. There were nine of us sitting around the
table; five in my aunt and uncle's family, and four in ours.
These were the survivors, and these were their children.
Except for my father's sister and her family in New York,
there were no others. As a boy, I was both aware and not
aware of the smallness of our group. They were the only
family I knew, and no one spoke of those who were absent.
What was the point?

But there were other unseen spirits at our seder. My
cousin took pleasure in secretly shaking the table, causing
the wine within *Eliyohu's kos* to lap the insides of the cup.
This was presented as evidence that the prophet's spirit
was among us. I was taken in by the deception which
made me anxious. I was already fearful of a prophet-ghost
who wandered from seder to seder. My angst reached a
climax when we opened the door to allow him to enter. I
hid, terrified he might actually show up.

Later in the seder, after the meal consisting of *kharoy-ses*, an egg with salt water, *gefilte* fish, with roe, carrots, jellied fish *yokh*, and *khreyn*, chicken soup with *kneydlekh* (the small, hard kind), some version of gray meat, a *pey-sekhdike kugl*, and *tzimmes*, I felt comforted. This feeling of well-being only increased after we broke out in Yiddish *peysakh* songs: *Tayere Malke, gezunt zolstu zayn*, a *peysakh* drinking song.

As *peysakh*s came and went, I grew less afraid of the *Baba*, and less afraid of *Eliyohu*. My fear was replaced by an empty sadness, a yearning for the ghosts who might have distracted me from the smallness of our seder table. It was a longing, perhaps, for even more than a brand-new tricycle, a *Baba* of my own.

Inheritance

"Take what you want." My sister slumped in the one available chair.

My father's studio apartment in Alphabet City appeared as I had imagined, a dilapidated sofa bed with cigarette burns on the upholstery, a chrome dinette table and matching chair, a four-drawer chest, and a single lamp in the corner. I hadn't seen my father in ten years and now he was dead.

Nothing in sight sparked my interest. I opened the single closet where his clothes hung. I ran my hand along the shelf above the clothes rack and found the multitool my wife, Ingrid, and I, had given him for his sixtieth birthday, just after our daughter was born. We saw the gizmo on TV. "Only $29.99. Call now. Operators are standing by." My

Originally published in Bright Flash Literary Review, May 2025

father was handy when he wasn't drunk. It seemed like the perfect gift.

I dropped it in a Gristede's shopping bag. A Planters Peanut can, blue, abraded in spots, sat on the shelf across from the tool. I reached for it, curious to see what was inside. It was heavier than I had expected, filled nearly to the brim with screws, nails, nuts, washers, bolts, of every size. There were oddly shaped pieces of metal as well, likely scavenged from contraptions that outlived their usefulness. I placed the can in the bag, thanked my sister for taking care of the arrangements, and left for my home in Yonkers.

"What's in the bag?" Ingrid, asked.

"You should've seen the place."

"The bag."

"Oh. I took back the tool we had given him years ago. Along with a can of junk he must have been collecting for decades." I removed each from the bag for Ingrid to see.

"He must've used that stuff to fix kids' bikes in the neighborhood. Remember your sister told us he did that from time to time?"

"Yeah. I remember him fixing my bike growing up." I retreated to the basement where I found a place above my workbench for the can and tool.

Two weeks later Ingrid called me into the kitchen and pointed at a cabinet drawer.

"The drawer pull fell off."

I inspected the knob, the metal shaft, and screw threads.

"The nut's missing. Did you hear it fall?"

Ingrid shook her head. I searched the drawer and floor but couldn't find the nut. I brought the drawer pull to my workbench in the basement and fumbled through my collection of screws and nuts which were neatly arranged by size in small plastic containers. None of the nuts fit.

"My father's stash," I mumbled to myself and tried to remember where I put the can. "There it is."

I emptied a portion of the contents onto the workbench counter with the motion of a gambler shooting craps. Then I sifted through the pile with my index finger and when a nut looked promising, I tested it.

"Damn. Close but no fit."

I rummaged through the contents of the can for another three or four minutes.

"Got it. A bit rusty but it works!"

I shoved the nut in my pocket and carefully guided the mound of rejected pieces into the can using the side of my hand. I climbed the steps to the kitchen, and replaced the drawer pull.

"You fixed it. Nice."

"With a little help from my father," I said, leaning against the laminate counter with my arms casually folded across my chest.

Ingrid looked baffled.

"I found a nut in the stupid Planters Peanut can."

Her expression did not change.

"The can of hardware bits and pieces I brought from my father's apartment?"

"Oh, yeah. I remember. Your inheritance."

Six weeks later, a similar thing happened. This time it was a hex screw I needed to adjust Ingrid's seat post on her bike. I returned to the can at least a half dozen times during the next year, and each time I found just the right part. I shared my observation with Ingrid.

"Uncanny," she said, raising her left eyebrow.

"Funny. What do you think it means?"

"What do you think it means?"

I shrugged.

A year passed. The unveiling of my father's gravestone was scheduled around the anniversary of his death. My sister had arranged for a simple inscription to be placed on the stone he shared with my mother; "Loving Husband, Father, and Grandfather."

"You left some things off," I whispered to my sister.

She glared at me, but her disapproving expression rapidly faded.

We were all gathered at the grave; my sister, wife, daughter, brother-in-law, nephew, and the rabbi we hired for the occasion.

"Would you like to say a few words?" The rabbi looked at my sister and me after reciting several psalms in Hebrew.

My sister cleared her throat. "Dad was a complicated

man. It wasn't always easy. My parents often didn't get along, but they loved each other. And now they're together forever. In peace, I hope. No arguments now about who will get the last word."

The rabbi suppressed a chuckle.

"Truth be told, my brother got the worst of it. He and Dad fought all the time." My sister turned to me. "But he loved you. He once asked me for advice on how he could make things better with you. I told him not to drink so much. He smiled."

"Rabbi, may I say something?"

Of course."

I told the story of how I went to my father's apartment after he died and found the blue Planters Peanuts can. I described what was in the can and how I always seemed to find just the right screw or nut or washer to fix whatever needed to be repaired. As I spoke, a quivering feeling started in my feet and climbed to my head. My eyes welled and tears streamed down my face and onto the crown of the monument. My sister, wife, and daughter embraced me. It was a perfect fit.

The Milos Viper

The Aegean breeze, gentle yet insistent, cooled my scalp through thinning hair. Waves of heat danced over the pumice shore. The resulting undulations evoked visions of ancient Athenian warriors weary from the Peloponnesian War, their swords dripping with the blood of island men. The downfall of these prideful islanders who would neither pay tribute nor surrender was so complete that their lineage teetered on the brink of extinction, save for the women and children spared only to be enslaved. The sorrow of these survivors weighed heavily upon me. Milos.

"Milos! I can't believe we're actually here!" Katie ran to me from behind and vigorously shook my shoulders with both hands.

Originally published in *BooksNPieces*, May ,2025

"Stop! My head's coming off." The protest was earnest. I was still suffering from jetlag.

"Can you believe these rock formations? They're pure white." Katie darted back and forth on the volcanic moonscape of Sarakiniko and took in everything she saw until she resembled a puffed-up frigatebird with her chest about to explode.

"Breathe. We have a whole week to explore."

Katie could not be contained. She ran up one mound and down the next. I tried to distract her.

"Hey, look!" I shouted. It was early morning so there were very few people around.

I motioned with my head toward a bent old woman on a nearby hill wearing a long black dress and kerchief that sharply contrasted with the chalk white cliffs. She was walking in the brush between the outcroppings, rhythmically bending over, grabbing vegetation, and placing handfuls in a straw bag.

"Didn't you say there might be snakes in the brush?" Katie had been terrified when she'd heard of the venomous creatures that inhabited the island.

"I guess she didn't get the memo about sticking to the walking paths," I shrugged. "She seems to know her way around."

"Where do people go if they're bitten? There's no emergency room. Just that tiny clinic in town." Katie's enthusiasm, brought to a boil by the Milos sun, was now reduced to a slow simmer.

"These snakes are peculiar." I was grateful to finally have Katie's attention. "You're not supposed to suck out the poison or apply a tourniquet."

"How do you happen to know this, Dr. Herpetologist?"

"World Wide Web. I looked up information about the island after arranging the trip." Unfortunately, my new-found knowledge had come just minutes after pushing the "complete booking" button on Expedia. I wasn't crazy about killer snakes either.

"Then what the hell are you supposed to do if one bites you?" Katie's voice had moved up half an octave.

The woman in black must have heard because she stopped harvesting and turned to look at us. As soon as I waved, she looked away.

"Something about an elastic band around the limb, but not a full tourniquet. Relax. You remember what the car rental guy said. 'Just stay on the walking paths.'" And with that, Katie and I walked back on the path to our car.

•

Katie and I had been together for twenty years. It was because of my parents that we never married. They were neither observant nor did they believe in God, but it would have broken their hearts had I married outside the faith. They liked Katie as much as they could, but an Irish Catholic daughter-in-law was of little use to them.

"Get rid of her," my mother commanded in a thick Yiddish accent. Never known for her loquaciousness, this proclamation was especially curt. "Katie is fine," she said another time, "just not for you." My father, sitting within earshot, kept reading his Yiddish Forward.

After visiting the beach, Katie and I returned to our rental house perched on a bluff overlooking the sea. It was the kind of place where you couldn't tell whether you were inside or outside. Magnificent lounge chairs bejeweled the deck. Each had an enormous, blue-and-white striped, terry-tufted pillow that swallowed you up so completely you neither could move nor wanted to.

"You look like you're ready for my famous raspberry ouzo slush," Katie offered, wearing only her capris.

"You think you're the Venus de Milo?" I stared directly at her bare breasts.

"Who cares? It's hot and no one can see us." Katie's defiance of convention always excited me. Her platinum blonde hair and blue head scarf fluttered in the breeze, resembling the Greek flag through my squinting eyes.

"Are we going to visit the site where the Venus was found?" Katie asked as she glided to the outdoor kitchen and began to prepare her alcohol concoction.

"If you want. I read there's nothing much there to see."

My eyes were still drawn to Katie's breasts.

"Eyes up."

"You only have yourself to blame," I turned and sank into the terry covered pillows.

"Here. Drink this. It'll cool you off." Katie handed me a tall glass filled with a ruby liquid and tiny beads of ice.

"Delicious." So glad I didn't get rid of her.

•

A gentle northerly picked up overnight and coaxed my eyelids open the next morning. My jet lag was gone; I had not felt so relaxed in years.

"Ancient or modern?" Katie asked, thumbing through her Fodor's Guide to the Cyclades. Today was going to be a museum day. "Actually, never mind. The archeological museum is closed. The war museum looks kind of interesting. It's in a converted German bunker."

"Terrific. That would satisfy my quota for a daily Holocaust reminder."

Katie smiled disapprovingly. How could I get rid of someone who understood me so well?

"War museum it is!"

We drove along a narrow road to Plaka. An English language sign beckoned us down a flight of concrete steps leading to two steel doors built into the side of the hill. There was no one around.

We sat on a weathered bench outside one of the doors. After half an hour, an overweight, middle-aged woman wearing a day dress and slippers lumbered down the steps. She was smoking a thin cigarette and wheezing as she rushed toward us.

"Are you here for the museum?" she asked.

"We weren't sure you were open."

"Three Euros. Each."

"You, ok?" Katie asked as we walked a long narrow tunnel-like hallway. She knew I leaned toward claustrophobic.

"Fine," I lied.

The entrance hallway led to a group of large rooms with vaulted ceilings. The walls were lined with photographs telling the story of Milos during the German occupation which lasted exactly four years and three hours, according to a sign, from May 9, 1941, to May 9, 1945.

"Who knew there was so much fighting here? It feels like Milos is in the middle of nowhere," Katie whispered.

"Hey, come look." It was a black cardboard exhibit with the photographs of fourteen young Greek men.

She read the poster.

"Allied planes torpedoed a German merchant ship moored in the harbor, it said. Fourteen German sailors died. The islanders were starving and gathered anything that drifted onto the beaches. Fuel, clothing, food."

"Oh my God," said Katie. "The commander of the Milos forces, Hans Kawelmacher, punished the locals for stealing by executing fourteen Melians on Aliki beach."

"German symmetry," I remarked to Katie. I tried to ignore the old tightness in my chest. "Let's get out of here." The smell of cigarette smoke grew stronger as we approached the open door, and we were met outside by the woman in the day dress and slippers. I was glad to be outside and feeling better.

"What did you think?" she asked.

The question was surprising. The emphysemic toll collector now sounded more like a docent.

"I didn't know about the executions. Those were war crimes."

She exhaled smoke in a satisfied sigh. "The martyrs were never buried," she said. "They were burned so nothing should remain. Whatever was left of them was eventually placed in a shrine across from the beach where they were shot."

"The German commander. What happened to him?"

"You mean Hans Kawelmacher. He never paid for his crimes. Died an old man surrounded by family and friends. And he was a barbarian even before he got here. While he was in Latvia he did all he could to kill Jews."

The tightness in my chest returned.

"He didn't kill Jews himself. He just ordered more troops from Germany so the exterminations could go faster."

I needed to change the subject.

"Were you related to any of the executed men?" I began to suspect her museum duty reflected a personal connection.

"Of course. Everyone in Milos is related."

•

"It's not my fault we can't find that damn taverna. It's supposed to be somewhere around here." I was exhausted by the rutted boulder fields that passed for roads. It was beginning to get dark.

"I'm not blaming you," Katie said.

Suddenly a figure emerged right in front of us, smack in the middle of the road. Although I was driving very slowly, I barely avoided hitting her.

The startled woman momentarily froze. I frantically fumbled with the door handle, but inadvertently pressed the lock button instead. By the time I was able to push open the door, she was gone.

"I think that was the woman we saw the other day on the hill with the snakes," I told Katie. My heart was still racing.

"The old woman in black?"

"Exactly." I was fairly certain. Same hunched posture, same black clothes, same straw bag.

"She went off that way." Katie pointed to a dirt trail that intersected the road.

We followed a few steps down the trail and could see it led into a ravine where a house stood in the distance. A single illuminated light fixture marked its threshold.

"Let's go. Little old ladies in black make me nervous," Katie said.

We resumed our drive. Both my hands tightly gripped the wheel.

"There it is. Finally." I pulled into a parking space in front of the taverna. "The guidebook said it had the best pitarakia, crunchy crescents of dough stuffed with manouri cheese and local herbs. I sure hope so, after all this."

The waiter seated us and brought bread and tzatziki for the table.

"Do you happen to know an old woman who dresses in black?" I asked him as he poured our water. "She seems to live just down the road. We encountered her a few times since coming to Milos." I thought it best not to share the details of our latest meeting.

The waiter smiled. "Everyone on Milos knows her." I expected him to continue, but he stopped.

"Can you tell us?"

"Yes, of course." Again, he paused, like a water pump that suddenly went dry. "It's...very sad."

Katie and I looked at each other, then up at him. Finally, he continued. "Her name is Maria Delis. Maybe seventy-five, maybe older. She is not good in the head."

"Not good in the head?" I asked. I had suspected something was off about her.

"She became...trelos...mad...during the war."

I took a shot in the dark. "Did she have a relative among the men executed by the Germans for taking things from the destroyed ship?"

"You know the story? No, not executed."

"Despina, come here. These people want to know about Maria. Despina, she's the owner, can tell you better."

Despina appeared to be about the same age as the woman in black. While our waiter stood by, she took an empty chair at our table.

"Maria and I were schoolgirls together. Like sisters. She married just before the Germans invaded. I had known her husband Georgios too, a long time. Strong, handsome. A fisherman like his father and brothers. He and Maria were sweethearts." She seemed practiced in recounting these facts.

Katie moved her chair closer to the small round table, her chin supported by folded hands.

"The morning after the attack on the German ship Georgios went to the beach together with his three brothers and many people from the town. The people gathered the things that floated in from the sea. Not the first time this happened. The Germans never did anything about it."

"Until this time," our waiter chimed in.

"Until this time," Despina repeated in a snarly tone, looking side-eyed at the waiter. "Maybe they were angry because the war was not going well. Who knows. This time they made arrests."

I knew all this from our bunker tour. "And what happened to Georgios?" I was listening so intently my feet were nailed to the floor.

"He was detained...along with his youngest brother, Nicholas. Nicky was only twenty."

One of my feet broke loose and began to tap uncontrollably.

"Maria was frantic. She heard there would be executions. She went to the German commander to plead for mercy for her husband."

I felt Katie's hand on my knee, squeezing harder with each of Despina's revelations.

"You can imagine what happened. Maria was a beauty. The commander did not hesitate to take advantage. They say he insisted that Maria must do it willingly and with affection. Can you conceive of such cruelty? Maria did what she had to do." Despina slapped one palm against the other in alternating fashion, as if she were removing filth from her hands.

"Then what happened?" Katie blurted out.

"Georgios, as promised, was spared. But Nicholas, God rest his soul, was not. Georgios pleaded with the Germans to shoot him instead of his young brother and could not understand why his pleas were not heard. He later learned the truth. Milos is a small island."

"I can't imagine how guilty he felt," I said.

"And angry. He could forgive neither the Germans nor Maria. He was a prideful man and though his wife had saved him, she had also brought him shame. They fought bitterly. He called her a 'Nazi whore.' At the end of the war, he left both Maria and Milos." Despina paused. She stared blankly across the room at a painting of the Virgin Mary with Child.

"And what happened to Maria?" Katie asked.

Our waiter took over. "Like I said. She became mad. She kept to herself and started dressing in black."

"We saw her working in the bushes near a beach the other day. Doesn't she worry about the snakes?" That was Katie.

"Snakes?"

"The vipers. They bite and are very poisonous."

"Ah...ochia! Yes, very dangerous. They say she has been bitten so many times she is...like vaccine..."

"Immune?"

"Yes, immune. But not immune from crazy. Maybe from sadness, maybe from snakes, maybe both. Have you decided what you want to eat?"

•

"I want to go to the beach," I told Katie the following morning.

"Sure. That was our plan," Katie responded, taking a final sip of her coffee. She was already wearing her bathing suit.

"No. I mean the beach."

"Oh, I see. I don't think it's very far."

We drove past what were now familiar landmarks

— downtown Adamantas, the Milos Mining Museum, the airport. There, on the left, stood a small white building with a cross atop the angled roof. A plaque in front listed the names of the martyrs, just as we had seen at the War Museum, along with their dates of birth and death. They were all in their twenties and thirties. Aliki beach stood directly across. The jade-colored Aegean washed over the shoreline, nudging grains of sand up to a sheer rock face some six meters high.

Katie and I stood staring in silence. The silence was broken only by the sound of the stiff breeze, the lapping of the ocean, and the passing of occasional cars.

"They were innocent." A voice emerged from the shrine. A woman walked from behind the building, matches in one hand, a memorial candle in the other. It was the woman in black.

"You are Maria," I said.

"Someone told you. I am famous here on Milos. 'The crazy old woman.'"

"You don't seem crazy to us," Katie responded. She had no basis for that assessment beyond politeness.

Maria looked toward the ocean. "The children laugh and call me 'Old Medusa.' They even make up silly songs about how I can turn them to stone with my stare. I love children, but they can be unkind."

"Yes," Katie said. "Not only children."

"Actually, the children have it backwards," Maria said.

"It is others looking at us that can turn our hearts to stone."

Katie and I looked at each other.

"The children are not entirely wrong. I have good days and bad days. I come here at least once a week. It helps clear my mind. My niece brings me in her car." Maria paused before the plaque and softly uttered a prayer. At the end, she made the sign of the cross three times, her hand closed in the traditional Orthodox manner.

"We heard the story of what happened to you during the war." I took a chance she would not be offended.

"Yes. I am hoping for a Homer to come along and create a real Greek myth about me! So much more reliable than stories passed down orally."

Self-deprecating sarcasm and a sense of humor. A woman after my own heart.

"Maria, how do you get along?" Katie asked. I loved her compassion.

"I harvest medicinal herbs. There is a good market for them in the cosmetic industry. I sell what I collect to a man who sells to companies. I don't know what they do with them, but they say the herbs make the skin look younger. Picking them, as you can see, has no effect." She pointed to her deeply wrinkled face.

Katie and I hesitated, then laughed.

"Follow me." Maria crossed the road, looking left, then right, for traffic. She led us down a path along an embankment to the beach. "This is where it happened."

I imagined myself blindfolded, standing against the rock wall. Better to face front or back? My heart began to race.

"Maria, you and I have things in common," I said, uncertain how this would be received.

Katie fired an incredulous look at me. Maria looked puzzled.

"Hans...the German commander..."

Maria's face blanched. "The Milos Viper." She spoke in an undertone barely louder than her prayer.

"That's what you called him?" Katie shuddered at the mention of the snake.

"That's what he was. We all called him that and worse." Maria turned to me. "You said we have something in common."

"Yes. We learned yesterday that the Viper arrived in Milos from Latvia, where he hastened the murder of tens of thousands of Jews. My father was from there. He was the only survivor from his family." I was shaking.

"I am very sorry for you and your family."

I saw the anguish in Maria's face. She took a few steps toward me and the anguish turned to calm.

"There is an ancient Greek expression: 'Those whom the gods wish to destroy, they first make mad.' Truly, I went mad. There were times I thought I would fulfill the will of the gods and end my life."

Maria's words landed hard.

"Time heals nothing, I learned," she continued. "But scars protect. Enough to go on."

"You wear black." Katie pressed.

"I mourn for them, not me. I am here." Maria again turned to me. "You and I are here."

My eyes welled up. I wished to be turned to stone.

"Do you have a name?" Maria asked as though she were my teacher on the first day of school.

"Simon. Named for my father's brother."

She nodded. "You are not mad, Simon, nor are you destroyed."

"No, Maria. Our families were. And through them, you, and me."

"We are not destroyed," Maria insistently retorted.

I looked away.

"You seem unconvinced, Simon. Tell me, what brought you to Milos?"

I had never thought about what brought me anywhere. I looked at Katie. "She did. I wanted to make her happy."

"She looks happy enough. And you, Simon?"

I could not raise the corners of my mouth, not even a little.

The northerly wind picked up. The sand on the beach began to blow in all directions, pummeling the rock face where the prisoners stood. We offered to drive Maria home.

"No. My niece is coming soon," she said. She led us up the embankment path toward the road. I heard the crunching sound of pebbles underfoot.

"Stop!" Maria commanded, raising her hand. A thick golden-red serpent, its diamond-etched scales radiant under the Melian sun, slowly slithered across the path in front of us, then paused. It was three feet long and its eye was as white as a pearl. "Not a sound."

Katie stood paralyzed, motionless except for her trembling lower lip. The viper's broad, triangular head bobbed up and down and from side to side signaling danger. Its tongue protruded and retreated, sparingly taking in scents from the intermittent gusts of wind. Maria stood directly in front of the viper. She maneuvered her hands like an orchestra conductor, first matching the movements of the snake's head, then slowing her hands until the snake's motion stopped.

"This should not be happening," Katie whimpered in a futile protest.

The viper turned its head toward me and opened its mouth, revealing its deadly fangs. I stared the snake in the eye.

"Let it pass," Maria said. She lowered her hands.

The viper continued across the path and disappeared in the thorny brush along the rock wall. The Aegean northerly, now blowing my hair straight back, swept the shores of Milos, stroking ash and rock.

On Account of a Talis

O ne Shabbos morning before *Rosh Hashanah*, Miriam leaned to Isaac and whispered: "Did you know that Rabbi Helfgot leaves the *bima* just before *Yekum purkan* every *Shabbos* and returns just before *Ashrei* so that he can go to the men's room?" It seemed a peculiar observation and Isaac answered her that he had never really noticed until she pointed it out. Isaac took the revelation as just one more piece of evidence of what a finely tuned human being the Rabbi was, a man of unassuming discipline and understated habit. The awkward image of the Rabbi doing his business lingered with Isaac for a moment, then gratefully disappeared.

Miriam and Isaac Shayvelson had never been shulgoers growing up but now assumed a place in their shul in the netherworld between the Shabbos regulars and the once-a-year, High Holidays crowd. For this, albeit less than fully pious commitment, they had Rabbi Helfgot to thank. True, having been the recipient of good fortune in their family on more than one occasion that they believed could only have come from divine intervention, they were ripe to join the community. But Rabbi Helfgot sealed the deal. He was a force; a righteous but pragmatic clergyman who knew how to deliver a sermon that hit the high notes but rarely stepped on too many toes. He was wise, kind, and able to make everyone feel at home. He won Miriam and Isaac over and they loved him ever since.

Rosh Hashanah was approaching, and Miriam and Isaac were looking forward to having their family together. Their children were now fully grown, in that window just before creating families of their own. The Shayvelsons arrived in shul the morning of Rosh Hashanah and showed their tickets to the security officers hired for the occasion. Isaac marched directly to the cubby where he kept his blue velvet *talis* bag which contained the *talis* he had purchased when his daughter became Bat Mitzvah thirteen years before. Isaac had never owned his own *talis* before then as he never really felt a need for one. The *talis* he wore on the occasion of his own Bar Mitzvah was a hand me down from his cousin. Both the *talis* and matching *yarmulke*, blue and white with pictures of Maimonides, the Wailing Wall, and other iconic images, were stored in a plastic bag in his top dresser drawer. Neither *talis* nor *yarmulke* was intended to be used again, but as remembrances of an important life passage, could not be parted with. Isaac remembered the day he purchased his *talis*. Uninitiated in such matters, he mustered his courage and journeyed to a Judaica store on the Lower East Side. A middle-aged, bearded Hasidic salesman, *peyes* wrapped around his ears, approached him. The salesman by his very demeanor and stance appeared confident that he could help each customer find just the right *talis* as easily as he could help find the right suit or shoes.   Certain the joke would be wasted on this throwback to the 19th century, Isaac smirked inwardly, thinking, "the *talis* chooses the Jew," and not the other way around. Isaac was overwhelmed by the choices, linen versus wool, Traditional versus Messianic, white versus color, black stripes versus blue stripes, geometric patterns versus images of Jerusalem, matching *talis* bag or not, with or without a biblical inscription around the collar, and on and on. Now Isaac understood that the "business" end of the *talis* resided in the four fringes sewn into each corner, the *tsitsit*, tightly grouped strings wrapped in a certain way hanging from the garment. These fringes were prescribed in the Bible as a reminder of the contractual binding with God. The rest of the *talis* is more or less "for show."   He tried some on, not knowing exactly what he was looking for. This one seemed too gaudy and likely to call attention to himself. That one, too Bar Mitzvah boyish.   Did he want to look like the kind of Jew who knew his way around a *siddur*? He finally narrowed it down to a choice of three relatively large woolen *talesim*, not quite beige, but off-white with simple black stripes, and a modestly ornamented collar without an inscription. This was the kind of *talis* that fell down your arms and you had to flip up and over your shoulders, the kind you could wrap yourself in. He had always thought this type of *talis* looked pretty cool, kind of old school. Compared to the no-muss, no-fuss *talis* that one wears around the neck and forgets about, this type of *talis* requires the wearer to grab a fistful of cloth in each hand every so often and toss the excess over one shoulder, then the other. "The difference between automatic and stick," the salesman joked. Isaac was caught off guard by the Hasid's decidedly modern sense of humor. The wool was warm and comforting around his body. He felt connected to generations of *talis*-wearing Jews before him, a *talis* he could wear for years in life and through eternity when the end came. He gave the Hasid his credit card, satisfied with his choice.

Rosh Hashanah finally arrived. Standing at his cubby on Rosh Hashanah morning, this year, coincidentally, a Shabbos morning as well, Isaac took this very *talis*, stretched it out by the collar before him, and kissed the collar three times. Next, he flung the *talis* around his shoulders, clasping the ends of the collar over his head with his outstretched hands while reciting the requisite prayer as he did so. He ended by flipping the excess material over his right shoulder and then doing the same with his left. He located his family and together they entered the sanctuary, service in progress, *siddurim* in hand. The Shayvelsons were among many families in attendance, as they looked around to see who was there, who was absent, who had grown, who had a new grandchild, who a new spouse. Isaac enjoyed the feeling of community, the sense of sameness he imagined among the families in attendance, and the davening. It made him feel secure.

Midway into the morning service, Isaac excused himself to go to the men's room. Because it is improper to wear one's *talis* in the restroom, the shul thoughtfully installed a long wooden fixture with many wooden hooks in the hallway just outside. Depending on the day, Rosh Hashanah being perhaps the busiest, the hooks often overflowed with *talesim*, sometimes two or three to a hook. Isaac was fortunate to find an empty hook, placed his *talis* there, and went in. On returning to the hooks several minutes later, Isaac looked to retrieve his *talis*. He did not see it immediately and began to rummage through the multitude of *talesim* thinking someone had likely moved his. No luck. He experienced a sense of rising anxiety in his chest, reminiscent of what he felt when he could not immediately locate his toddler child in a department store or supermarket. He thought that someone had surely taken his *talis* thinking it was his own. Because this error had certainly occurred within the preceding minute or two, he walked quickly through the crowded hallways of the shul, looking for some Jew who was now wearing his *talis*. Weaving and dodging his way adroitly, he took off to search. He scanned every *talis* in his visual field as he made his way, right length, wrong color, right markings, wrong collar. It seemed that whoever had mistakenly taken his *talis* had vanished into the repentant crowd.

Crestfallen, Isaac did not know what to do. Certainly, he thought, someone would soon recognize his mistake and return the *talis* to the rack outside the men's room. He waited expectantly but no one came. He decided to investigate further. On inspecting the *talesim* on the hooks, he noticed that one *talis* remained unclaimed. He examined it carefully and noted that it bore some resemblance to his own. Aha, he thought, a clear case of mistaken identity. But as he examined the *talis* in more detail, his anxiety grew. It was worn, a bit frayed, and had food stains on it. He surmised that the poor condition of the *talis* meant that the owner, and, presumably, the Jew who walked off with his own *talis*, likely belonged to the once-a-year, High Holidays crowd. As a "once a year guy," the owner almost certainly lacked a close relationship with his neglected *talis* and would not recognize its familiar "feel." In short, he might never realize that the *talis* he now had in his possession did not actually belong to him. Isaac's panicky feeling in his chest now drifted downward to become a sickening feeling in his stomach. Isaac grew depressed. In the darkness of his mood, he felt a sense of emptiness and violation. It seemed unfair that in the holy season of reflection and repentance, he should fall victim to such a circumstance. And the dark thoughts grew darker, as Isaac allowed himself to think that there might even be a *talis* thief in their midst.

There was little more Isaac could do at this point than select a "synagogue issue" *talis* off the rack outside the sanctuary. It pained him to do so. It was the first step toward an unthinkable conclusion that his *talis* was gone for good. Disgusted, he grabbed the *talis* closest at hand from the rack and threw it unceremoniously around his neck. It felt small and cold. He returned to his seat and whispered to Miriam, "I went to the bathroom and when I returned, my *talis* was gone." In his brief confession to Miriam, unexpectedly, he felt overcome with humiliation. He should have taken better care. There was nothing he could do but sit in his slippery plastic chair with his puny *talis* and resume his davening. He admitted to himself that his devotion now seemed half-hearted, unable to rid himself of his irritation and shame.

But Isaac was not one to give up, so he sat there conjuring a plan between penitential prayers. He would approach Rabbi Helfgot and ask him what he should do. The Rabbi on hearing the story would be sympathetic, no, outraged that such a thing could happen in his shul. He would make an announcement for all to hear, not accusatory, but heartfelt, yet fully conveying the desperation of an unnamed congregant who only wanted to be reunited with his *talis*. Surely, this would have the desired result. Isaac waited until the end of the service, waited for much of the sanctuary to clear, and nonchalantly approached the Rabbi according to plan. He greeted the Rabbi and they wished each other a healthy new year. Isaac delivered his news, expressing just the right proportions of distress and matter-of-factness. The Rabbi, to his surprise, seemed fairly unaffected by the story, sharing that a similar thing had happened to another congregant the preceding year, and no, the *talis* was never recovered. Isaac worked hard to suppress his discomfort on hearing this. The Rabbi ended with asking Isaac to remind him tomorrow, just before the sermon, and he would be happy to make an announcement. Remind him, Isaac thought? How could the Rabbi be so indifferent? Isaac felt worse and made his way home with his family.

He barely slept that night and returned to shul the next day to remind Rabbi Helfgot and hear the Rabbi's announcement. Short, sweet, and to the point. No sense of indignation. No conveying of urgency. Just the facts. By now, Isaac had elaborated his own ritual which he coined the *"talis* quest." First, check the hooks outside the men's room, then the cubbies where the regulars stored their *talesim* and *tefillin*, and, finally, the racks of *talesim* belonging to the synagogue. The latter felt like rummaging through Filene's Basement. The concluding prayers of Rosh Hashanah came and went, and still there was no sign of Isaac's *talis*.

Some say the days between Rosh Hashanah and Yom Kippur are the holiest of the year. Fully expecting to speak to God during these holy days, he never expected God would speak back. He was worried that God had sent him a message. Was it a warning or an omen? In either case, he was convinced it was a bad sign. No "Shayvelson, Isaac" entry in the Book of Life this year. Instead of preparing his soul by engaging in self-reflection and asking forgiveness from others as a prelude to asking the same from God, Isaac could not get the thought out of his head that there was a Jew somewhere wearing his *talis*.

Suddenly, as if jolted from some mysterious realm, a thought came to Isaac. What if this calamity was a test? After all, he considered, a *talis* is a thing, an object, cloth made from the very same dust as him. Wasn't he supposed to renounce worldly possessions in favor of the wellbeing of the soul, disavow things material in favor of service to God and his fellow man? The *talis*, he pondered, was not important in itself, but in what it represents. It binds him to God, no matter the trappings. A new sense of shame came over Isaac as he slowly unearthed yet another sin to be included in his conversation with the Creator. But with this revelation, the shame quickly turned to partial relief, as the loss of his *talis* felt less weighty around his shoulders. He had not felt this feeling of calm in days. And then, as if being irresistibly guided to some burning bush, Isaac had another insight. Perhaps the Jew who took off with his *talis* was in greater need of his *talis* than he? This was surely a noble and comforting thought. Transforming vengeance to virtue, Isaac mused that this was somehow meant to be, bashert, and, that he, Isaac, was better for the experience.

In fact, Isaac felt so inspired, he decided to share his revelation with Rabbi Helfgot. Although he knew Rabbi Helfgot would be very busy during in the days preceding Yom Kippur, he took a chance, and was able to make an appointment for Tuesday, following the Maariv service.

"So, what's on your mind, Isaac?" Rabbi Helfgot started, as he slowly took his seat behind his desk, weary from the weight of the season. "Did your *talis* ever turn up?"

"No, Rabbi, that's what I wanted to discuss with you," Isaac excitedly responded.

Isaac went on to recount the story of the *talis* in some detail but spent the most time elaborating the tumult he had been experiencing in this head, the panic of finding it missing, the guilt over allowing this to happen, the shame of thinking so negatively about some anonymous Jew, and finally, the return of peace stemming from an important lesson learned.

"And what was this lesson, Isaac? the Rabbi asked quizzically.

"Rabbi, I was too attached to the *talis* as a thing, a garment. I lost sight its true significance. A symbol of faith and devotion. Faith and devotion that I could possess with or without that particular *talis*. Nothing has been taken from me. I was given a gift." Isaac said triumphantly.

Rabbi Helfgot took this all in and looked at him deeply. Isaac was secretly hoping the Rabbi would incorporate his story and its important lesson in his *Kol Nidre* sermon for Yom Kippur. Isaac's story would be a modern-day example of the importance of *tzedakah*, not merely giving money, but offering the generosity of spirit, in the journey toward repentance. But instead of praising Isaac for his wonderful reframing of a trauma and unraveling what was no doubt a message from God, the Rabbi simply said,

"Yes," and looked at Isaac in a manner that seemed somewhat distracted. "Well, an important lesson indeed, Isaac. I hope your *talis* turns up. Have a good evening."

Isaac was flooded with emotion and could not comprehend this completely casual response. Did the Rabbi not understand the lesson here? Had he misjudged Rabbi Helfgot after all? Isaac did not know what to do or say, so he got up to leave. Just as he was leaving Rabbi Helfgot's study, he caught the image of a *talis* just out of the corner of his eye, folded, resting on the Rabbi's blue velour sofa, partially hidden under a pillow and some texts. It looked a lot like his. So accustomed to approaching scores of *talesim* over recent days in order to check them out, he had to fight hard to resist the urge to do so again in the moment. Resisting what felt like an irresistible gravitational pull, Isaac forced himself to leave the study without breaking stride or drawing attention to himself.

"Good night, Rabbi, and thank you," he remarked as he headed down the stairs and out the front door of the shul.

He was consumed by this fleeting image of the *talis* on the sofa as he walked home. Had someone returned the *talis* to the Rabbi's study and the Rabbi not know it? Unlikely. The Rabbi was aware of all things, or so it seemed. Could this actually be the lost *talis*? Most likely, not. He could only know by unfolding it, examining the markings, feeling its size and heft. In short, he would have to wrap himself in the *talis* to know for sure. He had to know for sure.

Isaac could not resist the compulsion to examine the *talis* he had just eyed. He walked around the back of the shul, past the small sanctuary entrance, and secreted himself by the large weeping willow tree that stood behind the Rabbi's study. His plan was to wait until the lights went out, then let himself into the shul. Isaac knew that the Rabbi never locked his study. The main trick was to get into the shul just before the security officer left for the evening. So as not to arouse suspicion, he would make some pretense about having to check something out upstairs, and slink into the study. Isaac suddenly saw the study go dark. He made a beeline to the front of the shul, waved at the security officer mumbling "I'll only be a minute," and bounced up the stairs. Without any wasted action, illuminated by a lone light in the outer office area, Isaac grabbed the *talis* on the sofa, handled it, looked at it, and checked its size by throwing it around his shoulders. There was no doubt. This was his *talis*. But what to do now? Without further hesitation, he snatched the *talis*, folded it loosely, placed it snugly under his arm, and took a step toward the door. As if blocked by a mysterious force, however, he could not take a step further. He felt the tension grow in his shoulders, his hips, his legs, as he struggled with his locomotion. "Why can I not take what is mine?" he murmured to himself. No answer came. He placed the *talis* on the Rabbi's velour sofa where he found it and suddenly felt free to leave. Isaac staggered home confused and at a loss. Despite the turmoil he felt in the Rabbi's study, Isaac slept well that night.

Kol Nidre came and went a few days later without further incident. In the busy holiday season that followed, Isaac's annual religious fervor and resolve which always started strong, gradually diminished. Although he no longer lamented the loss of his *talis*, he could not bring himself to buy another and settled on using the synagogue issue.

A year passed and Rosh Hashanah was coming up quickly. "Early this year," Miriam noted. Isaac, Miriam, and their children attended Shabbos services just before the start of the High Holidays. Isaac sat in the slippery plastic seats toward the back of the sanctuary, but nevertheless noticed that Rabbi Helfgot excused himself from the *bima*. Inexplicably, Isaac suddenly remembered what Miriam had told him a year before about the Rabbi's habit of using the men's room at just this time during the Shabbos service. Just as inexplicably, Isaac decided to follow him.

Isaac exited the sanctuary and saw the Rabbi walking down the long corridor toward the men's room. He followed the Rabbi at a safe distance. The hallway was crowded so Isaac stood on his toes to make sure he did not lose sight of the Rabbi. From a distance, he saw the Rabbi place his *talis* on one of the pegs outside the men's room. Instead of going inside, however, the Rabbi turned adroitly on his heel, and deftly took a different *talis* from a nearby peg. He wrapped it around himself, walked further down the hall, and then disappeared up the staircase leading to his study. He returned within a minute or two, this time with what appeared to be yet a different *talis*, a third *talis*, around his shoulders. Isaac was dumbfounded. "What was happening here?" he said to himself in a hushed tone. The Rabbi took off this third *talis*, entered the men's room (Isaac would not follow him in), and soon emerged. The Rabbi then took his original *talis*, wrapped it deliberately around himself, and left the third one right next to where his own had hung. Curious, but also a little afraid, Isaac glided over to the hanging *talis* outside the men's room and reached for this third *talis* the Rabbi had left. His heart pounded as he immediately realized this was the very *talis* left in place of his own the previous year, somewhat worn, frayed and complete with food stains. Isaac turned pale.

It was confirmed. The Rabbi was the culprit. Isaac thought to turn the Rabbi in, but to whom? To the president of the shul? The cantor? The police? None of these alternatives seemed appropriate. Confronting the Rabbi was also out of the question. So, Isaac kept his discovery to himself.

Isaac and his family attended Rosh Hashanah services that year as usual. Mid-day, just after the president of the shul gave his annual address, thanking the clergy, the officers, the ushers, and the staff for all their hard work to make this day possible, and just before the sermon, the Rabbi stepped up to the podium. It was Rabbi Helfgot's custom at this time to announce the schedule for the day, when parents should pick up their children, and so on. It was also now that the Rabbi made his odds and ends announcements.

"If you own a blue Volvo, license plate 847BLP, your lights are on. Also, if anyone found a missing Jerusalem *talis*, beige with vertical gold stripes, with the *tsitsit* blessing on the *atara*, please bring it to the *bima*. Thank you."

Isaac smiled inwardly, recognizing Rabbi Helfgot's handiwork.

And on each Shabbos, when the Rabbi would disappear from the *bima* for just a few minutes between *Yekum purkan* and *Ashrei*, Isaac Shayvelson would turn to Miriam Shayvelson and whisper, "There goes the Rabbi." Miriam would glance to Isaac and complete the rejoinder, "to the men's room. To do his business."

"No doubt," Isaac responded, gently caressing one of the *tsitsit* hanging from his borrowed *talis*.

Closets

"**D**o you want to hide in your closet?" Micky asked Sandra, his friend, down the block.

"Why would I want to do that?"

"It's dark and quiet and no one will know we're there!"

Sandra shrugged. "OK."

Micky followed Sandra into her bedroom and opened the closet door. It contained only a few dresses, two pairs of identical polyester pants, one in red and one in green, a heavy wool cardigan, and well-worn white Mary Janes on the floor.

"Are these all your clothes?" Micky asked.

"No. I have the rest in the dresser over there."

Micky walked into the shallow closet and sat on the floor. He told Sandra to sit next to him and then he reached up and closed the door. A stale odor of sweat and leather rose from the Mary Janes, but Micky didn't mind. The two six-year-olds sat in silence for a few minutes.

"What happens now?" Sandra whispered.

The question had never occurred to Micky.

"Sometimes when it's really quiet, I can hear ringing in my ears," Micky offered.

"Oh," Sandra said, looking puzzled. "How long do we sit here?"

"As long as we want." Micky could not understand why she was in such a rush to leave. "Now comes the best part."

"What's that?"

"When you open the door and the cool air hits your face," Micky said as he pushed the door open. "Feel that?" Micky could tell from Sandra's smile and wide eyes that she thought it was the best part, too

•

Micky first discovered closets when he was four. Standing outside his New Jersey row house, he'd grabbed a handful of pebbles from a deep crack in the sidewalk to see how far he could throw them and accidentally struck the grill of a parked Chevy wagon directly in front of him. The sound of pebbles on chrome resonated like so many marbles dropped on a tin roof. Certain he had caused terrible damage, he ran into his house, flew up the stairs, and hid in the small closet in his room. He sat there in terror for a very long time until he realized no one was looking for him. The air of his room greeted him like the chill from their Frigidaire.

When Micky wasn't hiding in tight dark spaces, he liked to sit on the stoop of his house with his favorite possession, a plastic green water pistol. He happened upon the toy while walking down his block one day and finding it near his neighbor's trash can. It worked great at first, but eventually began to leak. After that, he had to refill the gun as quickly as the water leaked out using a small, dented saucepan. The best he could do was pull the trigger and squeeze a few drops of water mixed with air. On such days he sat there expressionlessly, the useless water pistol in his hand.

"Vat ya doin, Milty?" His father had just come home from work at Roebling Steel, a job Leo would say he got "thanks to the Nazis."

"Not Milty. Micky."

"OK, Micky."

"Nothin," Micky responded without making eye contact. "My water gun's broken."

"You shouldn't play mit guns."

Micky focused on his father's deformed hands, the knuckles permanently swollen. These too had been gifts from the Nazis.

Micky refilled his pistol with the little bit of water

remaining in the saucepan. His father walked past him, up the steps and into the house, shaking his head in disapproval.

"Esther!" Micky heard his father yell up to his wife, the way he did every night when he came home from work. He heard him trudge up the staircase to the bathroom on the second floor and cough up phlegm.

No one called Micky to the table for dinner. No one had to, so unvarying was the routine. As soon as Leo got home, Esther put out a quarter of a cantaloupe for each diner and returned the remaining quarter to the refrigerator. The appetizer was followed by a *klops*, a large gray meatball cooked in onions without sauce, or occasionally roasted chicken. Alongside the meat was a baked potato cut in half. A bottle of Heinz ketchup was available for the *klops* or chicken, and a stick of Fleishmann's margarine for the potato. For dessert, there was *kompot*, Del Monte's fruit cocktail. Micky saved the red cherry halves for last. No one spoke.

After dinner, Leo lay on the living-room floor in front of the TV, hands behind his head, with his feet perched on the steps to the bedrooms to relieve the swelling in his legs after a long day standing at work. No one disturbed him during the *velt nayes*, the world news. Focusing on the news allowed the effects of the thinly disguised Jew-hating taunts from his coworkers to recede. The men at the plant especially liked to make fun of his Yiddish accent. At least once a week Esther and Micky heard about "*der daych,*" the sadistic German foreman at Roebling who condoned these regular abuses.

"Relax, Leo. They don't mean nothin'. It's all in good fun," *der daych* would say.

Leo never complained or spoke back at the factory. He needed the job. Esther grew silent on hearing these incidents and Micky scampered off to pee.

•

Leo and Esther were sweethearts before the war and survived the camps together. Separated at Ravensbrück, they were sent to the same subcamp, where Esther was put to work forging British currency and Leo built aircraft for the Luftwaffe. Despite the risks of communicating, the two managed to keep tabs on one another. Their eyes met at the morning count. Sometimes they were assigned jobs in adjacent workshops. They pooled their food scraps when they could.

Liberation came and went. Broken people, Leo and Esther were splints for the other. They moved aimlessly from DP camp to DP camp until good fortune finally came their way and they made their way to America in 1949. Trenton, New Jersey.

"Trenton makes, da voild takes," Leo was fond of saying. "That's vat it says on da bridge when you drive in. Such a city. Such a country!"

It was time to start a family because the family they had was mostly gone. They managed one child, a son, Milton. The boy was named for Leo's father Mendl, who was thought to have been gassed in Sobibor along with his mother Rokhl, though no one knew for sure. Esther's sister *Khave*, the only other survivor in the family, had arrived in Vineland, New Jersey with her husband a year before. Chicken farmers.

"Milton is a fine American name," *Khave* advised the couple before the *bris*. But after a few years of merciless taunting from the neighborhood's Billys and Sallys and Pennys and Johns, Milton told everyone his name was Micky.

Leo and Esther were as adept at parenting as they were at naming their son. Esther couldn't hold the child comfortably; she kept adjusting the position of her arms, never finding the sweet spot. The baby's helplessness frightened her. When he cried and could not be comforted, she did not know what to do.

Milton drank from his baby bottle well into his third year. He continued this way even when the last rubber nipple cracked, and it began to leak milk down the fat folds of his neck.

"Again mit der bottle?" Leo reprimanded Esther when he got home from work. His son was reclining in front of the Philco black and white, watching Looney Tunes and sucking on his milk.

"He's so stubborn, a real *akshn*," she said. Esther had tried to take the bottle from Milton on many occasions. Each time he would desperately carry on, kicking and screaming, like a tenacious calf unwilling to give up the teat.

"I...WANT...MY...BOTTLE! I...WANT...MY...BOTTLE!" This tirade went on in an incessant, sing-song whine, so loud the neighbors could hear. The struggle often ended when he crawled on all fours to his mother's nylon stockinged feet. He rubbed them with his hands, then caressed them with his face and nose, inhaling whatever comfort he could, sobbing as he begged. Esther gave in and that was that.

Leo glanced at Esther and saw her defeated expression.

"Don't vorry, he von't haf a baby bottle under da *khupe*."

After dinner, Leo would take over the TV watching, focusing on the world news with Walter Cronkite. He was amused that the anchor's surname meant "sickness" in Yiddish. After the sign-off, Leo would do his own take. "And dat's da vay it is," he'd say.

•

"Mommy?" asked Micky the day before school was to start. They were in the kitchen; his mother was ironing boxer shorts.

"Vat is it?"

"I'm afraid to go to first grade." He looked at his scuffed

shoes, then at her bare stockinged feet.

"Dare's not'n to be afraid of. It's just school. You'll get used to it."

He hadn't gotten used to kindergarten. He had the teacher with the reputation of locking children in closets. One day, too afraid to ask his teacher for permission to use the boys' room, he peed through his husky corduroys. "Come here," the teacher beckoned when she saw his wet crotch. Micky's eyes fixed on the coat closet. But no: the teacher reached into the closet for an oil cloth, an item meant to protect tabletops from kindergarten hazards, and wrapped it around his waist. He was humiliated. And he didn't make a single friend all year. Once, during recess, when he was about to drink from the communal water fountain in the schoolyard, Micky heard a voice from the line of kids behind him waiting to drink.

"Hey kid, your mother's callin'!"

Micky pirouetted. She wasn't there. The prankster slashed ahead and greedily gulped water from the fountain. Micky's face flushed. He looked for his mother again, then back to the fountain. The spouting water could not quench his thirst.

"How can I go to first grade?" Micky asked his mother. "I don't know anything!"

Esther shook her head. "Dat's vie you go to school."

"I don't know how to read," Micky pleaded. All he'd done in kindergarten was finger paint.

His mother put down her ironing. "Deddy and I learnt to read in night school and ve didn't even speak English," she replied. She returned to the boxers on the ironing board in front of her, and Micky went out to the stoop, his water pistol and saucepan in hand, trying to squeeze every drop of water he could from his broken gun.

•

Esther, unaware that mothers accompanied their children to school on their first day, sent Micky off to first grade on his own. He approached the school building and saw kids with mothers and even a few with both mothers and fathers. His heart beat faster as he navigated the forest of parents holding their children's hands and engaging in playful conversations. Pinballing into adults and children, not knowing where to go or how to be, made him dizzy. Eventually, the parents left, and the children were asked to form lines according to the grade they were entering. He took a breath, the first, he thought, in a long time.

Micky was assigned to Miss Temple's class. "She's so young," he heard a girl sitting next to him say. "I heard she's nice," another girl twittered. Micky noticed that she smiled a lot, even when she spoke. He loved it when Miss Temple gave him one-on-one time at his desk. She crouched low so the edge of her dress just touched the floor and cocked her head toward his, helping him sound out the words.

"'Let's go for a walk," said Alice,' his teacher read by his side. "Now you read the next line."

"'Can...Spot...come...too?'" Micky read.

"Excellent, Micky! Your reading is really coming along." When Miss Temple said "coming along," she meant it could be better. But Micky didn't care much what she said. The smell of her hair, just inches from his face, was exhilarating.

His nervousness about school quickly dissipated. In no time he could read like the other kids. He started hanging out with a group of boys at recess, the smarter boys in the class, and developed a reputation for being good at dodgeball. One evening he showed his spelling test to his mother.

"Another A. Very nice, Milton." Micky's mother called him Milton on such occasions.

"I'm going to be a 'Great Jewish Leader' when I grow up," Micky blurted out. He got this idea while staring at the Goldberg Funeral Home calendar. November had a picture of Moses on Mount Sinai holding the Ten Commandments, brilliant light shooting from his head toward the heavens.

"Very nice, Milton." A barely perceptible smile crossed her lips, but then quickly disappeared.

As Micky gained friends, he learned more about his classmates and their families.

"When are we going to buy a car?" Micky asked his father.

"'Vat? Da bus isn't good enough for you?"

Micky carried on and would not let it go just as he had not let go of his baby bottle.

"Do you know vat a car costs?"

Micky had no idea.

Truly, Micky's family did not need a car. They rarely went anywhere. He heard boys at school talk about driving to a restaurant to eat. He asked if they could do that, too.

"My food isn't good enough for you?" his mother asked.

"Do you know vat ve ate in da cemps? *Shtayner!*" Leo shouted. Micky's Yiddish was good enough to understand they ate rocks. And that was the end of any talk of cars or driving to restaurants.

•

The next afternoon, Micky's mother's face turned ashen as she placed the handset onto the receiver of the black wall phone. "Your fadder hed a heart attack at voik today." She collapsed into a kitchen chair and broke down sobbing.

Micky started crying too. He didn't know what a heart attack was, but it sounded like a very bad thing. He ran to his mother and threw his arms around her. She didn't stop crying, and she didn't hug him back. Standing by her chair, Micky caressed her shoulder. They remained this way for a very long time until his mother finally gathered herself and stood up from her chair.

"I'll make you dinner den I'll go to da hospital," she said, wiping her tears. "You'll stay mit Sandra and her mother."

"But..."

"Da hospital doesn't let children visit."

The dinner routine and hospital visits continued for a week or so until his father came home. Micky learned an unfamiliar word, convalescence. It meant his father had to stay in bed for months and needed complete rest. He was only allowed out of bed to use the bathroom. Everything else would strain the heart that had been attacked.

"Stop benging mit da ball!" his mother would yell. "It makes such a recket! You'll disturb your fadder!" To Micky's ear, "disturb" from his mother was like Miss Temple's "coming along." It meant Micky was likely killing him. Micky had always assumed his father was safe from attack since the Nazis had gone, but now he understood that he and the Nazis had some things in common.

For months, Micky lived with the burden of thinking he had contributed to his father's condition. After all, the attack happened the week after Micky had brought up the car and the restaurants. He assuaged his guilt by waiting on his father hand and foot. He brought him his meals. He brought him his *Jewish Daily Forward*. He helped change the bed linens. Knowing his father could not go down the stairs to watch the world news, Micky would watch Walter Cronkite in his place and report back to his father every evening.

"Such a voild," his father would say. "Tomorrow breng me betta news."

Micky had not said a word about his father's situation to Miss Temple or anyone at school. When Miss Temple gave the class an assignment to make a drawing of a chore they did at home, Micky drew his father in bed while he stood at the foot, a tray in his hands.

"Micky, what's that you've drawn?" Miss Temple asked.

"I bring my father food and stuff because he can't do it for himself since his heart..." Micky started to well up.

Miss Temple put her arm around Micky and walked him to the hallway. She told him what a heart attack was. She said it was probably because his father smoked too much and had had a hard life. When they re-entered the classroom, she hung his drawing on the bulletin board next to all the others. "It is clear that Micky loves his father very much to take care of him that way," she said to the class. Micky wiped his tears.

The assignment turned out to be preparation for asking the students to take on chores in the classroom. Miss Temple called it "good citizenship." The list of jobs was long and included chalkboard eraser clapper, plant waterer, goldfish feeder, bulletin-board manager, fire-drill officer, show-and-tell master-of-ceremonies, pretzel-stick merchant, size-order monitor, and sashes boy. Micky's ears perked at the announcement of the last job.

Sashes were a special kind of closet where the students hung their coats, jackets, sweaters, and anything else they brought with them to school. They were the mother of all closets, consisting of floor-to-ceiling overlapping panels that travelled in heavy-duty grooved runners. They spanned the length of the classroom, and considerable force was needed to push the panels opened and closed. This, Micky thought, was the perfect job for him. He boldly raised his hand to volunteer.

"Micky, you would like to be the sashes boy?" Miss Temple asked.

Suddenly, a second hand shot up.

"Timmy, you are also volunteering for this job?"

Timmy was a tall, awkward Irish boy with a freckled baby face, red hair, and a reputation as a troublemaker. Miss Temple decided the sashes could use the combined strength of the two, so both he and Timmy were appointed sashes boys.

Timmy's interest in being a sashes boy soon became clear. At the end of each day, Timmy would shove Micky into the closet, close the sashes, hold them closed, and let out a high-pitched giggle. Micky played along and feigned distress. After a few minutes Timmy would open the sashes to find Micky quietly sitting on the floor. Timmy would leave with a stupid, self-satisfied smile on this face.

Until one day when the prank became serious.

"Hey Micky. Let's stay in school after everyone else is

gone. We can run around the halls, look in our teachers'
desks, and do whatever we want. Whaddaya say?"

Micky was tempted but wary.

"Are you chicken?"

"No."

"This is the plan. When the dismissal bell rings, make
sure you and me are at the end of the line. Instead of leaving the room, we run for the sashes and hide."

"OK." Micky was still nervous, but it sounded simple
enough.

●

"BRINGGGGG!" The bell sounded and off they went.
They waited a while in the sashes until the coast was clear.

"Let's go," Timmy whispered and opened the sashes.
He shoved Micky in and abruptly shut the panels. Micky's
head hit the back wall.

Despite the headache, Micky sat calmly on the closet
floor as usual, occasionally demanding his release. But five
minutes, ten, fifteen passed, and Timmy had not let him
out. The closet was not airtight, but it was stifling and hot.
The ringing in Micky's ears became intense. He banged
on the panel. "Come on, Timmy. Let me out!" he yelled.
"This isn't funny anymore!" Ten bangs, twenty bangs. No
response.

Micky tried with all his strength to force the sashes
open, but they would not budge. He tried kicking the panel
open but could not get leverage to generate enough force.

He felt around the dark closet for anything he might use to help him get out. Nothing. But in the very corner of the closet his hand hit upon a shoe, then its mate. They were high heels, probably Miss Temple's. She sometimes wore shoes like that when parents or the principal came to visit. Otherwise, she wore her usual flats. He held one shoe in his hand, brought it to his nose, and sniffed the insole. Then he did the same with the other. The odor of leather and foot was soothing. The ringing in his ears stopped.

It was time to get out, for real. Micky shifted his body so he could press his back against the plaster wall and kicked the sash panel with both feet. After five such blows, the bottom of the panel exploded out of its runner, and he was free.

Timmy was standing there, the moonlight from the tall windows illuminating his rageful glare.

"Look what you did, you Jew-boy jerk!"

"What I did? You're the jerk!" Micky retorted. Micky had never been called a Jew-boy. The words triggered a fury he had never experienced. "Say you're sorry!"

It was clear Timmy had no such intention. The stupid smile returned to his lips.

Micky jumped the bigger boy and threw him to the ground. He punched him in the stomach over and over again, and in the face for good measure. It was only when Timmy began to beg for mercy that he stopped. As soon as he did, Timmy jumped up and ran from the classroom.

Micky, exhausted, returned to the closet and lay on the floor, cradling Miss Temple's shoes in his arms.

•

Leo was home in bed as usual. Now Esther was working to keep the family afloat. Good with her hands, she'd found a job as a saleswoman at Fishman's Jewelers on State Street and quickly learned to do simple watch and jewelry repairs. Still, her salary was only half of what Leo had earned.

"I hev to get back to Roebling," Leo said when she came home from work and checked on him.

"We can't survive on just your pay."

"You need to rest," she reminded him. "And after all, ve got through much voise."

"Yes, but dat vas before ve had Milton."

She looked around. "Vere is Milton? Maybe at Sandra's?" She prepared dinner, as she always did, job or no job. Thirty minutes went by and still no Milton. "That's funny," she told Leo. "Milton is alvays home by dinnertime. I'll go get him." But when she buzzed Sandra's apartment at the building on the corner, Sandra's mother said she hadn't seen him. And he wasn't outside on the street or on anyone's stoop. "Maybe the school will know someting?" she asked Leo. She turned off the oven, leaving the mostly cooked chicken inside, walked the six blocks to the school, and rang the bell. An elderly Black man with gray hair and matching beard came to the door.

"Help ya, Ma'am?"

"Tank you. I am looking for my son, Milton. He is in Miss Temple's class. He never came home."

"The children left hours ago. And the teachers too. The kids call me Pops. I'm the custodian."

"Can ve look around? Maybe someting heppened to him."

The two walked up and down halls, stopping in the gym and auditorium, calling out his name.

"Let's try his classroom," the custodian said. He led Esther up a flight of steps to Miss Temple's room, unlocked the door, and ushered Esther in. At first, when he turned on the lights, nothing seemed amiss. Then he saw a boy's legs protruding from inside the sashes.

"He's in here!" he said.

The voices woke Micky. He threw the shoes he'd been cradling in his hand to the corner of the closet and sat up, legs crossed, squinting because of the brightness of the light in the classroom.

"Mom?"

"Vat heppened to you?"

Micky proceeded to tell his mother and the custodian the whole story—except the part about what he did to Timmy.

Esther turned to the custodian. "Tank you Mr. Pops...I don't know vat ve vould have done if not for you. Milton, let's go home and tell your fadder you're ok."

Micky, still sitting on the floor of the closet, got up slowly and followed his mother out of the classroom.

"Mommy, wait. I forgot to tell you something. Timmy called me a Jew-boy jerk. I made his nose bleed."

Esther's shoulders slumped. "Good."

"What did he mean?"

"He doesn't like Jews."

"Why?"

Esther stopped. Micky couldn't see her face but heard her whimper. This was the second time he had seen his mother cry. He clasped her hand in his. The calendar image of Moses and the Ten Commandments flashed through his head.

Esther released her hand and wiped her tears with a handkerchief she pulled from her bag.

"Your dinner will be cold." She continued walking down the hall.

"Thanks for coming to get me, Mom."

"Dat's vat mudders do."

Like ironing and making *klops* and buying husky pants, Micky thought.

Micky followed, head bowed, several steps behind.

"And dat's da vay it is," Micky muttered to himself as they left the building. The cool night air rushed over his face.

House Money

"**I**'m not going to make it!" Jeb yelled at Lenore. His skis and poles were clasped in both hands at odd angles. He shuffled as fast as he could in his clunky Nordicas but did not want to draw attention to himself. The couple had reached the nexus of Zermatt's main gondola system by nine thirty but had not yet decided where they would ski that day.

But he did make it. His white Fruit of the Looms revealed a tell-tale line of clear perspiration instead of the brownish-blackish mess he had feared would be there. Jeb finished his business and emerged from the WC. His face was contorted.

"You alright?" Jeb thought Lenore's tone sounded mildly annoyed.

Zermatt had been the couple's dream ski destination during their thirty-year marriage. Both attorneys, Jeb and Lenore, could afford nice vacations.

The stimulation brought on by the combination of exercise and café au lait was more than Jeb's bowels could manage. He hated it when the urge to defecate occurred on the slopes. His Fila ski pants, Spyder jacket, turtleneck, heavy fleece, and thermal underwear made the dash and doffing sequence a particular challenge.

"Could have been a real disaster. Why can't this country build more toilets? So much for Swiss hospitality."

"Are you feeling up to taking the gondola?"

Jeb grabbed his skis and poles and marched off determined to force his body to comply. He walked toward the queue that was forming at the Matterhorn Glacier Paradise gondola with its access to the highest skiable peak. Lenore followed.

The two rode up alone in a gondola car that could accommodate six. Lenore removed her mittens and helmet. Jeb followed suit. They took in the scenery, Lenore looking down the mountain, Jeb looking up, but said nothing to each other until they passed the tree line.

"These snow fields are amazing," Lenore commented, turning her head just enough to see the enormous, open terrain to her right.

Jeb, not daring to jinx his GI tract, curtly muttered his agreement. He felt exhilarated by the vastness of the scene, all the while trying to keep his peristalsis in check. After a quick mental inventory of his self-soothing repertoire, he chose a personal favorite, radical acceptance. "If I poop, I poop," he thought to himself. Resigned to his fate, a small burst of flatus emerged just as the gondola doors opened in the summit station. It was a false alarm, a release of pressure. He felt better.

Pleased with this turn of events, Jeb noticed the clouds to his right suddenly lifted, and there before him stood the Matterhorn in all its grandeur, the bend of the peak resembling the face of a cloaked monk. He whispered "hallelujah." His eyes drank in the expanse of the mountain with the same relish he had consumed the Whymper Stube fondue special the night before. The pears smothered in cheese were delicious.

The two exited the gondola car. After a few lumbering steps, they retrieved their skis from their slots on the outside of the car and marched to the start of the trail. The sound of boots clamping into bindings mingled with the whirl of a brisk wind at the top. The views combined with the thinness of the air to take Jeb's breath away.

Before long, Lenore and Jeb were barreling down the slopes, carving S-turns in the nicely groomed, solidly intermediate slopes. They paused to rest after coming to the end of a perfectly groomed run.

"How are you feeling now?" Lenore asked.

"Cold."

"Cold is good."

"Let's stop for some gluhwein."

•

"Jeb, did you move your bowels today?" the nurse's aide asked, popping her head into his room at Empathium, the hospice he entered in his seventy-eighth year after learning his pancreatic cancer had spread to his brain.

"Yes, thank you. Would you like to see?" he said, pointing to the bedpan under him.

The aide rolled her eyes.

"I'll be right back to help you with that."

"You're an angel, Molly."

Lenore had died of breast cancer two years before. It had been a downhill spiral since then. His daughter, Rachel, their only child, was a litigator in California, where she lived with her husband and two children. She came east to New York as often as possible, more so in the wake of her parents' illnesses. Jeb was grateful for her help and affection.

Jeb did what he could to ease his anxiety about facing the end. Seeking comfort, his waning mental attention focused on the time he started dating Lenore. It was the seventies. Their favorite place was the Fort Lee Diner just over the bridge. Each booth had its own mini jukebox, and a quarter bought you three songs. Jeb played his memories like oldies.

There was no going forward. He could only look back. He had pushed the Zermatt button and there it was. He could push any button he wished.

•

It was Rachel's eleventh birthday and there was a customary gathering of the clan. Jeb, Lenore, and an assortment of Rachel's aunts, uncles, and cousins were in attendance.

"How many times are you going to tell that stupid story, daddy?"

"It's a good story," Jeb argued.

"I'll tell it," Rachel interjected. "You and Mommy wanted a baby—me—so bad, but just couldn't make it happen. Finally, you went to some fancy-shmancy doctor on the Upper East Side and did something that finally worked."

"It was a miracle." Jeb could not help himself, looking to Rachel with the same eyes as the day she was born.

"Shh. Don't interrupt. So, this doctor made 'a miracle,' and Mommy was finally pregnant. You thought your troubles were over, but they were only beginning. Do I have it right so far?"

"Perfect, honey."

"So, everything was going along fine until one day Mommy started cramping and bleeding. You rushed her to the emergency room, and they said, 'It's not good.'

Mommy had to stay in the hospital for a very long time. The doctors were not sure what to do. They argued with each other. They started medicine, they stopped medicine, they started medicine again. Mommy kept bleeding. They told you not to expect too much."

Jeb's eyes well up. "They told us you wouldn't make it."

"Relax, Daddy. You know how the story ends. And then ... and then ..."

"Another miracle."

"Shh. Yes, another miracle! Mommy stopped bleeding. But she—and I—were not out of the woods. She got diabetes. She got high blood pressure. They told you she could die at any moment. Finally, they decided I'm big enough and cut Mommy open. And there I was, just under three pounds."

"Sopping wet."

"Oh yes, I forgot. Sopping wet! I went to the NICU. Mommy went back to her bed. You went home. The end."

"Not quite. You left out the part where we took you home. You were so little, and your mother and I were so afraid something would happen to you. We were crazy."

"Mommy said you were crazy."

"Yes. I was crazy."

•

"I could use a little more morphine, Molly. Can you

please tell the nurse?"

"Of course. Is there anything else I can do for you?"

"Well, I'm having some trouble getting this jukebox to work," Jeb added.

Molly had been with the hospice for twenty-five years. "Let me help you with that."

"I put the quarter in. I'm entitled to hear one more song," Jeb complained. "I just can't seem to find the right button to push. "

"Well," Molly continued, "what is it you want to hear? Maybe I can find the button."

"I'm not sure. Try J4."

"Ok, Jeb. Pressing J4 now."

•

"They'll have to come out," Dr. Wyman explained to Jeb's mother. "They're huge and inflamed and need to come out."

Jeb was in the waiting room, but just within earshot of his mother and the doctor.

"He's only six. And he's so afraid of needles and doctors. Do you think he'll be alright?" Jeb's mother pleaded, looking for another way.

"He'll be fine, Mrs. Harrison. The doctors at Children's are very experienced at removing tonsils. They do it every day."

Jeb's mother exited through the waiting room where

Jeb was sitting quietly but in some discomfort. His throat was on fire. She took her son by the hand, walked to the bus stop, and waited.

"What has to come out, Mommy?" Jeb asked, finally having the courage to speak up.

Jeb's mother crouched so her face was just a few inches from his. She took his hands and placed them in hers. "The doctor said you need to have your tonsils out. You know, like Cousin Isaac."

"What about Rachel? She went into the hospital right after her birthday and never came out." Jeb looked away. He knew the mention of his sister's name would change his mother into someone he did not recognize.

"Sweetheart, that was completely different."

Jeb was surprised his mother responded.

"Your sister had a terrible accident. The doctors tried but couldn't make her better. She was very, very sick." Rachel, three years older than Jeb, had tumbled from her bike two years before and suffered a head injury that could not be surgically repaired.

Jeb's mother stood up from her squatting position and turned to see if the bus was coming.

"It's gonna hurt. I'm afraid." Jeb pulled away from his mother.

"I understand you're afraid. What frightens you the most?"

"Needles."

"They have to give you a needle for the medicine that makes you sleep, so you don't feel anything. They take you to the operating room, and before you know it, you're in your own room in the hospital eating ice cream. Daddy and I will be there with you the whole time."

"In the operating room?"

"No, they don't let parents in the operating room. But we'll be waiting for you as soon as you wake up. Promise."

"OK. What flavor ice cream do they have?"

"Whatever flavor you want."

"Strawberry. I want strawberry."

"Then it's strawberry you'll have."

The bus arrived and Jeb and his mother got on.

Molly waved goodbye.

Blackjack

It was the early eighties and only shadows of Atlantic City's once-vital boardwalk remained. You could still dodge blue motorized rolling chairs moving silently across warped wooden Boardwalk planks. Mr. Peanut still greeted you among the cracked shells under your feet, detritus dropped by six-year-old boys excited to gulp the warm nuts inside. Ecstatic screams still emanated from the piers, Steel and Million Dollar, with their scramblers, bumper cars, and Ferris wheels. And there was still a chance you could inhale the delightful aroma of chocolate when you happened past the open door of Steel's Fudge. The casinos brought in new hope and excitement, at least during the decade that followed.

"Hit me. Again. Again. Again."

"Twenty-one," the dealer said in a matter-of-fact tone that had just the right tinge of practiced exuberance.

"Amazin,' ma'am. Five card Charlie. You have the luck of the Irish." A balding man with sweaty hair, the local kibitzer, clutched his empty gin and tonic.

Tillie sat head-on-head with the dealer. Her eyes fixed on a spot on the green felt fabric just above the five cards, and her body was motionless except for the rhythmic tapping of her right index finger on a single black hundred-dollar chip.

The dealer paid Tillie the chips she was due, then cleared the table from the previous hand. Tillie neatly piled her winnings, keeping them separate from her play stack.

"Place your bets," the dealer announced as he dealt cards from the four-deck shoe face up to the players and a single card, face down, to himself.

"Hit me."

"Eighteen." The kibitzer mumbled.

"Stand."

The dealer drew a four, then an eight, and showed his hole card. Jack of spades.

"Bust!" the kibitzer blurted. "Tillie. You win! You always win!"

Tillie, in her sixties, had enough of the game and the bald man with sweaty hair. No longer concerned about separating piles, she swept her chips with the side of her hand into her oversized black handbag. The kibitzer watched just as he had done before. Instead of cashing out, Tillie kept walking past the roulette table, past the slot machines, through the lobby, and onto the boardwalk. Where she went after that, no one could say. It was the same every day.

•

Tseshe, a full-bosomed girl of eighteen who had always been meticulous about her appearance, did not mind the rain, even if the wetness exposed the outlines of her breasts. She was grateful for the opportunity to rinse off the stench of Auschwitz and had already become accustomed to the Kapos and SS guards staring at her with wide eyes, hateful and red. She, together with a work group of women, were headed back to Barrack 10 after their usual eleven-hour day of moving rocks from one place to another and then back again.

"Please...*bitte*...don't hit me," a fallen prisoner directly behind Tseshe begged. Her voice could muster neither strength nor desperation. What remained of her body lay in the road, unable to move. Tseshe and a fellow prisoner instantly picked up the woman and supported her weight between them. The beating would have certainly killed her. They dragged her back to camp.

Once in the barracks, the women took their places on the excrement-stained paper stuffed with moldy hay that passed for mattresses. They slept four to a berth, alternating head to foot, and stacked three berths high. Women who were too weak or too sick or both slept on the floor.

The smell of dysentery was everywhere.

Tseshe watched as two of the newer arrivals with remnants of color remaining in their cheeks removed a board from under a mattress and placed one end on the foot of the bed and the other on a windowsill. They sat down at their make-shift table and began to play cards. Afraid to make a sound, the two used hand motions. They called the game "*eyn-un-tvantsik*," twenty-one in their native Yiddish.

One woman said to the other, "How did you get these?"

"I traded for lipstick."

"Lipstick?" The woman's mouth gaped as though she had been told her friend had smuggled an elephant into the camp. "Why would you bring such a thing to such a place as this?"

"I didn't know what this place was. They didn't find it. I just forgot about it."

"And the cards?"

"I was by Barrack 24...where the women there...not Jews...survive by..."

"Yes. I heard."

"They needed lipstick. I needed food. They didn't have food, but they had a deck of cards. They told me I could trade the cards for food later."

"And how did you get the cards past the guards?"

"You know...inside."

"Deal."

Tseshe watched and listened intently as the two women played. She was trying to make sense of the game by looking at their pantomimed reactions and gestures.

"Would you like to play?" The owner of the cards had seen Tseshe staring.

"Why not."

Tseshe sat on the floor next to the woman who had been shocked by the lipstick story. "The point of the game is to get as close to twenty-one as possible without going over. Picture cards are ten, aces can be one or eleven. There are other rules, but let's keep it simple for now."

The owner of the deck dealt. "You're supposed to stand if you get seventeen or above," she said.

Tseshe got a jack, followed by an ace.

"*Eyn-un-tvantsik!*" the dealer said in a hushed but excited voice.

"Can't get off to a better start than that!" the other woman chimed in.

The three women played into the night. Tseshe won more than her share of the hands. Although it meant nothing, she liked how it made her feel.

The next morning, there was a roll call as usual. The head Kapo stood across from the women of the barracks. An SS officer stood ten paces behind him.

"Step forward when you hear your number called,"

the officer shouted. The Kapo translated into several languages. The prisoners did not need to look at their tattoos. The numbers were branded in their brains.

"4...2...7...3...6...0..." The woman with the cards stepped forward.

"4...2...7...3...6...1..." Her friend did as well.

Tseshe was waiting for her number to be called. She closed her eyes and stopped breathing for what seemed like several minutes. When she opened her eyes, she saw the Kapo give her an almost imperceptible nod.

The women who taught her to play were never seen again. These queens of hearts and diamonds went up in smoke.

●

Tillie sat down at her usual table the following day at her usual time, 9:00 AM. She preferred to play alone, which was not a problem at this time of day. She wore a rather ill-fitting gray dress with long sleeves secured by a cloth belt attached to the garment.

The dealer across from her was about to finish her shift. She clapped her hands and showed her palms in the traditional rotating motion Tillie had witnessed thousands of times. Tillie slipped her a toke even though the departing dealer had not dealt her a single hand. The departing dealer thanked her while the new one took her place in a seamless exchange.

"Good morning, Tillie." All the dealers knew her.

"Good morning."

The dealer motioned towards Tillie to place her bet. Tillie responded by removing a fifty-dollar chip from her betting pile and easing it into the betting circle.

Making a sweeping gesture, the dealer withdrew cards from the shoe. Blackjack. The dealer paid her a hundred-dollar chip.

The second hand was dealt. Two tens. Tillie held up a V with her middle and index finger, the sign to split.

"Hit me." Nineteen. "Hit me." Twenty one.

The dealer played. Bust. Tillie won again.

A woman in her twenties, disheveled, wearing last night's stained blouse and a much-too-short skirt, sat down in the anchor position. She placed her four chips haphazardly on the table but motioned the dealer that she was not ready to play.

"How's your luck today?" The woman arranged herself in her chair.

Tillie did not respond.

The woman glanced at Tillie's stack. "Looks like you're doing pretty well."

The dealer looked directly at the woman. "Place your bets." Appreciative of Tillie's always-generous tips, the dealers protected her.

The woman placed a twenty-five-dollar chip in the circle. She stood at thirteen and lost. She slid forward the second twenty-five-dollar chip, then the third. The results were the same. She was down to her last chip.

Tillie turned to her. "Place it in my circle." The woman obeyed.

"Blackjack." Tillie handed her three chips. "Now get out of here and get something to eat."

"Thank you. I will." The woman tottered away in her stiletto heels, one foot overlapping the other as though she were walking down a runway.

"Hard night," Tillie murmured. The dealer contained a half-smile

•

Days rolled into months and Tseshe was still alive. She somehow survived typhus and was assigned to an easier work detail, sorting the clothing of the gassed prisoners. Although she felt fewer aches and pains, the gnawing in her stomach never ceased. Not quite skeletal, she had lost, she estimated, a quarter of her body weight. Somehow, she could talk herself into enduring the lice and the diarrhea, but not the hunger. Throwing herself onto the electrical fencing was a thought that never left her.

Back in the barracks after a day at the clothing stacks, Tseshe found herself thinking about the card players. Their clothes might be in Mannheim or Frankfurt, she thought. She wandered to the place she had learned to play *"eyn-un-tvantsik"* and noticed that a floorboard was loose. Curious, she dislodged it and was surprised to find the deck of cards she was sure had vanished. She shoved the deck into the pocket of her dress. Knowing their origin and their value, she thought to go to Barrack 24 to see if she might exchange the cards for something to eat. A Kapo had noticed her, and she would use this. It was risky, but she was starving. They would go after the evening feeding.

"Would you consider accompanying me to Barrack 24?" She could barely get the words out.

"Barrack 24. That's an interesting destination."

They left that evening as planned. The Kapo hit her with his stick as they walked to make the scene convincing to onlookers.

After they arrived at the barrack, Tseshe went inside.

"What's that you got?" asked a woman wearing red lipstick.

"Cards...a complete deck."

"I know whose cards those are. She got knocked up and disappeared. What do you want for them?"

"Something to eat. A potato perhaps."

"A potato?" The woman in lipstick suddenly noticed how gaunt Tseshe looked. She was, nevertheless, attractive.

"Tell you what. We need some help here. Would you consider it?"

Tseshe grew numb. "They don't permit Jews."

"Who's a Jew? Were you circumcised? You are Tillie, a grammar school friend from Krakow. We were baptized in the same week and had our first communion together. Remember? Besides, you have blue eyes and light hair."

Tseshe could not take in what she was hearing. She would not be hungry, but at such a price.

"I have never had relations."

"You will learn fast...like we all did. You have your own room. A real bed. It's warm. And there is plenty to eat. And you get time off during your monthly."

Having lost so much weight, she no longer had periods, nor would she likely get pregnant, but no one had to know that. Tseshe made her choice.

"What about my number?"

"You'll cover up. Besides, it's dark."

"If I don't go back to my barrack, they'll know I'm missing."

"I have friends. We'll tell them you were taken to the hospital barrack and died."

•

The offshore evening breeze stridently blew across the white sands and boardwalk until it struck the casino edifices and swirled, lifting empty popcorn bags and skirts. Tillie emerged from this breeze and entered the Tropicana. No use searching for an empty blackjack table tonight. The city was dead mid-week, but this was a Saturday night during the height of the season, and the casinos were teeming with work-week refugees from three states.

A waiter dressed in a flowered shirt and white chinos approached her for an order. "What'll it be, Tillie?" She was entitled to a comped drink.

"Vodka on the rocks. Thank you."

"Comin' right up."

Tillie cased the casino looking for a first base seat. She found one just as a customer was leaving. It was still warm. The kibitzer, cleaned up for Saturday night and no longer sweaty, was in the seat next to her. The dealer instantly recognized Tillie and slyly winked so the pit boss couldn't see.

"Place your bets."

Tseshe was at evening roll call, the gallows with empty nooses swaying in the wind. Tillie waved the dealer off.

"Place your bets."

Now it was Sunday evening, when the officers preferred to stop by 24. Tseshe floated above her body. Again, Tillie waved the dealer off.

"Tillie, you know the house rules. It's crowded tonight. You need to play or give up your seat."

Tillie placed several chips in her circle.

Twenty-three. Bust. Nineteen. Dealer showed twenty. Eighteen. Push. Twenty-four. Bust. And so, it went for Tillie until her wager stack was down to two chips. She placed these in her circle. As she did so, the first two digits of her tattoo were exposed. Bust.

"Looks like your luck ran out," the kibitzer whispered.

Tillie pulled down the sleeve of her blouse and turned to the man with an amused smile. "Hardly," she said, as she retrieved a spare chip from her bag, toked the dealer, and disappeared.

The boardwalk was empty, and the offshore winds had subsided. There was a hint of salt in the air. The moon was the only source of illumination. That huge disk rested where the night sky met the sea, like a celestial chip waiting to be placed.

The Curse and the Cat

Harold and Susan, along with their seventeen-year-old daughter and twelve-year-old son, lived next door to a witch. Their neighbor generally kept to herself, but what few interactions they had were nasty. For example, when the recycling bin Harold's daughter put out one day was blown over by a fierce wind and the debris landed on the neighbor's lawn, the witch became irate and retaliated by making Amanda's face break out in acne. It was hardly Amanda's fault, but the actions spoke volumes about the temperament of this sorceress. Fortunately, these incidents were infrequent and of little consequence, so, in the interests of neighborly peace, Harold's family just put up with them.

Harold was a reasonably successful pharmaceutical representative and Susan a highly reputable endocrinologist. Everyone assumed they met in a professional capacity, with Harold calling on Susan in her office. Not so. The truth was they met by magic. Or, more precisely, the magic act both happened to attend in the theater of the Luxor Hotel where both happened to be at separate professional conferences. And in a turn of even greater coincidence, or let's call it karma at this point, each came onto the stage when the magician asked for two volunteers from the audience. Harold was to make Susan disappear through the miracle of magic, with some assistance from the magician on the stage, and then just as wondrously reappear. This interchange led to drinks in Vegas, a date in Philly, an enchanted courtship, and marriage. And when it came time to have children, although there were plenty of sparks and drive, they ultimately had to rely on the magic of IVF.

Amanda started life as a "good egg," a status that only blossomed over time. With her blond hair and blue eyes, she resembled Susan from the start; they grew to look like sisters. She was a good student, a good friend, a good kid.

Noah's Petri-dish start was likewise uneventful, but things turned topsy-turvy before he took his first breath. His was a breach birth complicated by a compromised cord. His first Apgar score was worrisome. He perked up by the time of his second several minutes later, but the doctors still feared that Noah might have suffered mild hypoxia for the first few minutes of life.

Apart from the fact that Noah seemed a bit fussier and feistier than his sister as an infant, Harold and Susan did not notice much difference. Their birth trauma worries dissipated over time.

They were wrong to grow complacent.

Noah was a quiet boy but mischievous in his own way. School was a struggle: his teachers and parents frequently noted that his work habits and scholastic performance compared unfavorably with those of his older sister. Noah was also a frequent visitor to the principal's office. He talked too much at the wrong times, made provocative comments, and often invoked the ire of his classmates.

"Is that a new dress or a Halloween costume?" Noah asked a girl in his class who was new to the neighborhood. The girl was reduced to tears, and her mother complained to the authorities. Noah thought this would be funny, an icebreaker, but realized, too late, it was not.

Noah wasn't a bad kid. To the contrary. He was a "one-man" anti-bullying campaign and was known for his coming to the aid of the small, the weak, and the easily teased. Of course, given his poor judgment at times, even his efforts in this arena proved self-destructive. The problem was, he didn't know when to stop pummeling the bully.

Amanda steered clear of comparisons between her and her little brother and provided support when she could.

For their parts, Harold and Susan tried to help Noah shore up his school performance and "behavior problems" by hiring tutors and enrolling him in a variety of sports programs to provide an outlet for his "excess energy." These interventions proved largely unsuccessful.

When Noah was in middle school, his parents consulted a child psychiatrist who met with Noah weekly. Noah liked seeing Dr. Handler; he seemed interested in understanding Noah's perspective on things. The therapist diagnosed Noah with Attention Deficit Disorder and recommended neuropsychological testing and medication. The testing revealed attentional and "executive function" deficits that Dr. Handler hypothesized might have been related to Noah's birth trauma. Noah started the medication Adderall; it helped but had some unpleasant side effects. Dr. Handler also diagnosed depression, which was not obvious to his parents and teachers, and which the doctor believed was related to Noah's feeling he was "bad."

On hearing all this, Harold and Susan felt they were "bad" as well. They had been too hard on Noah. They had waited too long to fully understand Noah's struggles, and this too had left him scarred.

•

Noah was doing better toward the end of middle school. One could even say his transformation was magical. When he was given accommodations that helped him manage his cognitive limitations, he was able to pause more consistently before acting, and he developed friendships that were satisfying. His grades also improved. The witch next door remained a fixture in the family's life. So did her black cat.

One winter day, Susan returned home from the market only to realize she had forgotten to buy avocados for the guacamole she had planned to make. Intending to make the five-minute drive back to the market, she got into her car in the driveway, put the transmission in reverse, lifted her foot from the brake, and slowly moved backward, not realizing that the neighbor's cat had parked itself beneath the family car to enjoy the warmth of the engine. She instantly heard an unearthly sound like the shriek female felines make at the end of mating, as they pull away from the male's barbed organ, but a thousand times worse. The sound lasted only a second; then there was silence. Susan was afraid to leave her car to investigate.

She didn't have to. The witch next door, both hearing the disturbance and perceiving the abrupt termination of her telepathic communication with what was not a pet but a familiar—her confidante, protector, healer, and spiritual guide—rushed to the scene. The witch howled, tore at her hair, punched her face, and darted back and forth in a state of utter agitation and horror.

Susan reluctantly stepped out of her car and took in the devastation she had accidentally caused. Her natural inclination as a physician and compassionate human being was to try to console her neighbor. But Susan did not appreciate the depth of the loss, and witches cannot be consoled in moments such as these any more than mothers can in the incomprehensible moment, they experience the death of a child.

Susan took a step toward the witch. The witch recoiled, then slowly hunched over, gently gathered up the remains of her familiar, and walked back toward her home. Susan watched her neighbor retreat, feeling empathy for this witch for the first time.

"I am truly sorry," she said, as both women retreated.

"I won't forget this," the witch blurted. "You and your family will be cursed come the morning." She pried the door of her house open with her right foot, her hands occupied with grief, and closed it behind her in the same way.

Harold knew something was wrong as soon as Susan entered the house. Her eyes were wide and wild, and she soon began shaking uncontrollably. She told Harold in a whisper what had happened. "What do you suppose she meant by cursed?" Susan asked, barely able to get her words out. Their neighbor had never used the "curse" word before.

Harold reminded Susan of some of the mild inconveniences they'd experienced before: Amanda's acne incident, the time the witch caused their house to smell like rotten eggs for a week after Noah accidentally shattered her kitchen window, the family of bats in the attic. "Let's just wait and see," he said. "Chances are it won't be so bad." He knew he was whistling in the dark.

The next morning was warm. The sun's rays shone through the windows and filled the house. Susan, awake earlier than usual, showered and went out to retrieve the newspaper from her driveway. All that remained of the previous evening's events was a small patch of red next to the rear wheel of her car on the driver's side.

From the bedroom window, Harold observed Susan's body tense upon investigating the scene and watched her run into the house with the paper clutched firmly under her arm. He could hear her scurry around the first floor. He then heard her bolting up the stairs to the master bedroom, where Harold was beginning to dress.

"I don't see anything out of place," Susan said. "Oh. The kids' rooms. I didn't check the kids' rooms."

She walked briskly down the hall and stopped at Amanda's door. It was Saturday and the children always slept in. Taking a deep breath, she opened the door slowly and quietly. Amanda was there, in bed, her blanket moving up and down with each breath. Susan exhaled.

Harold, going in the opposite direction, approached Noah's door. It was partially open as usual. Harold opened it further but did not see Noah. He walked to the bathroom the kids shared, opened that door, but there was no one there. Harold's heartbeat faster and he motioned Susan who was just coming out of Amanda's room to come quickly.

"Did Noah have a game this morning or was he getting together with friends?" Harold asked Susan in a peripatetic cadence.

"Not that I know of," Susan responded. "He's not in his room?" Harold shook his head.

Harold and Susan both rushed in to check again. They looked under the bed, in the closet, everywhere, but Noah was nowhere to be found. Looking at one another in cold silence, they heard a soft, high-pitched cry. It was the forlorn meow of a cat, and it was coming from Noah's bed.

Noah's heavy woolen blanket moved slightly and from underneath emerged a smallish calico cat, mostly coffee-colored with patches of white fur along its flanks and a splotch of black fur over its right eye. Neither Harold nor Susan had seen this cat before nor could they begin to imagine how it got into Noah's room, with doors and windows locked throughout the house.

"Do you think Noah brought this cat home?" Susan asked...

"No way. He knows I hate cats, and he knows I'm allergic." The presence of the cat momentarily distracted Harold from the anguished mystery of Noah's whereabouts.

Amanda was awakened by the tumult. She said she

had no idea, either, where Noah could be. The three got on their respective phones and called every friend of Noah they could think of. They called his teachers, his soccer coach, relatives in town. No one had a clue about Noah. In a moment of desperation and resolve, Harold nervously walked next door to speak with the witch. He rang her doorbell, then rang it again, but there was no response. No lights were on.

No sign of activity within. He placed his hand on the doorknob of the witch's front door and tried to enter. It did not budge. He was disappointed, but also relieved that he did not have to confront the unpleasant woman.

Hours went by. Some family and friends who had been contacted earlier that day stopped by for updates. When night fell and Noah was still missing, Harold decided to call the police. Officer Hogarty and his partner arrived at 8PM and took the requisite information from the family.

"When was he noted to be missing? Height? Weight? Hair color? Eye color? Distinguishing features? What was he wearing when last seen? Did he recently have an argument with anyone? Is there anyone who would want to harm him? Did he use drugs? Did he have any medical problems? Is there anything else you would like to tell us?" The interview went on and on. It was at this point that Susan hesitantly related the events of the evening before, the cat she tragically but accidentally ran over, the fraught interactions with her neighbor, the witch, and the curse.

Neither Officer Hogarty nor his partner placed much stock in witches or curses, but they had both heard of such things. So, they listened and decided to pay the witch a visit. The result was the same as Harold had earlier in the day. No one answered the door. They inspected the outside of the house, the backyard, the storm cellar door, and convinced themselves no one was home.

"Let us know if she returns and we'll come by to talk to her," the two officers said as they handed Harold a copy of the missing person's report.

"Oh, one more thing," Harold blurted out as they were halfway out the door. "We found a cat in Noah's room this morning. No idea whose cat it is or how it got there. Thought you might want to know."

"Thanks," Officer Hogarty replied. "We'll add that to the report when we get back to the headquarters." Hogarty rolled his eyes at his partner, and his partner responded in kind.

The family was alone now. Except for the calico cat they had forgotten about until Harold mentioned it to the police. Realizing it had not eaten all day, Amanda went up to Noah's room to bring it down to the kitchen, where she put out a bowl of milk and a plate of Bumblebee tuna. The cat followed Amanda instinctively and ate and drank with a vengeance. Harold went to the garage where he found some leftover cat litter they used for traction when the driveway iced over and put it in a box for the cat. Harold,

Susan, Amanda and the cat, exhausted, went off to bed.

The days went by and there was no sign of Noah. The family took to searching the neighborhood, then the surrounding towns, the city, in ever-widening circles. Not knowing exactly what they were looking for, the routine of searching gradually shifted to the routines of ordinary life. Harold and Susan eventually returned to work and Amanda went off to college. And the cat lived the life of a cat. Slinking around the house from windowsill to windowsill, sofa to lounge chair, occasionally stalking the odd bug. But every night, the cat ended up in Noah's room and curled up in his bed. There was talk of giving the cat away or placing it in a shelter, but the talk never went anywhere. And neither did the cat.

Curiously, Harold became his favorite, nestling on his lap at every opportunity, allowing his caregiver to endlessly rub the scruff of his neck. Rubbing the cat's neck was one of few things that calmed Harold and sustained him in the dark moments. And even more curiously, Harold's lifelong allergy vanished.

What also vanished was the witch next door. Weeks went by and her house remained abandoned. The police returned once or twice but had no leads as to Noah's whereabouts. Despite the return to more or less normal functioning, grief settled into Harold's and Susan's home like a thick layer of dust.

Susan cried for hours at a time. "I can't go on," she

sobbed. "Not without Noah. How can I live, not even knowing if he's alive or dead?" Susan's words were barely discernible under the pressure of her desperate sobs.

Harold, of course, shared his wife's feelings. All of them. But he did allow himself to be as demonstrative.

"Susan, listen to me. Noah will turn up. He'll be ok, and so will we. I'm convinced of it." Harold didn't believe it, but he felt stronger when he felt he was supporting Susan.

"We were always so worried about Noah," she said as she compulsively arranged the left-over missing person flyers on the coffee table in front of her. "Remember? And so hard on him. We never gave him a break. 'Study harder.' 'Go see this tutor.' 'Concentrate!' 'Why can't you be like Amanda?' Susan mindlessly moved the neatly stacked pile of posters from one end of the table to the other.

"We never let up, Harold. We're the curse, don't you see it? We were the witches. And now all of us are paying for it," Susan continued with less grief and more clarity.

Susan's words rang true, but the self-blame for Noah's disappearance did not sit well with Harold. "Susan," he said, "we aren't perfect parents. We made mistakes. We didn't know Noah couldn't do the things we wanted him to do. We wanted him to be successful, strong, and it worked. Look how much he changed. He's a great kid and we contributed to that too. I miss him, Harold." Susan was too spent to cry, too spent to argue.

186

"I miss him too." Harold and Susan went to bed, each facing their respective wall.

•

Harold woke up the next morning with the disturbing thought that the calico, who had become a fixture in the household, did not have a name.

"Susan, I think we should name the cat," Harold announced to Susan even before brushing his teeth.

"Whatever." Susan couldn't care less.

"I think I will name him..." Harold had already confirmed the cat was a tom... "Mulligan."

"Why that?" Susan snapped, surprising Harold with her sudden interest.

"I don't know. Just like the sound of it." Neither Harold nor Susan was of Irish descent, nor did they play golf, making the choice even more peculiar. "Mulligan it is."

The void created by Noah's disappearance did not perceptibly contract despite the passage of time. For Harold, caring for Mulligan provided small islands of relief in a mostly hidden tempestuous sea of angst. Susan, Harold observed, was drowning, with little to buoy her.

Three months had passed since they last saw Noah. Harold was preparing milk and Bumblebee in the kitchen for Mulligan's breakfast, as usual. He spoiled the cat this way, secretly wishing he were doing the same for Noah.

Mulligan typically responded to this attention by affectionately rubbing up against Harold's leg, releasing a gentle meow, and digging into his meal. This morning, however, it was different. Instead of the meow, Harold swore he heard the cat speak. While busily lapping at the milk, Harold pulled Mulligan away from the dish, gently took both his ears into his hands, and placed his own face inches from the face of the cat.

"What did you say?" Harold demanded. A stranger looking on would have thought the man had lost his mind.

"I heard you say something. What was it?" Harold paused, letting go of Mulligan's ears.

The cat looked up at Harold and said, "Dada." It was unmistakable. Harold fell back onto one of the kitchen chairs and watched and listened in amazement as Mulligan's face transformed into the face of a human infant, wailing all the while, as if he could feel the distortions in one part of his body, then another. It was as beautiful and magnificent as it was grotesque. Mulligan seemed not to be suffering in this process, as fur changed to skin, legs to arms and paws to hands and feet. The tail was the last to go. There was a child laying on the floor in front of Harold, speaking words in a rudimentary fashion. And the child, unmistakably, was Noah.

Harold, convinced he was hallucinating or delirious or both, was unable to utter a sound or move from the spot. But the transformation, it turned out, was not complete. The child, now clearly a toddler of two or so, was continuing to grow. Hair, facial features, torso, everything, everything expanded before Harold's eyes. Harold thought to reach out to embrace the boy, but Noah was growing too quickly, and he did not dare interfere with the bizarre metamorphosis he was witnessing. In the end, he wanted his boy back, healthy, in one piece. Safe. So, he let the process run its course until it stopped.

And finally, it did stop. It was Noah for sure, at about age five. Confident the bulging and popping had stopped, Harold reached for the child, picked him up, caressed and hugged him for what seemed like an eternity. He walked deliberately toward the living room where Susan was reading the paper and having her coffee. She saw Harold out of the corner of her eye and imagined he was carrying Mulligan, as he often did. Harold stood at the threshold of the room and simply said, through tears:

"Look what I found."

Susan, not expecting much, turned to see. When she realized it was not Mulligan at all, she jumped off the sofa. "What is it?" she asked...

"Noah," Harold said quietly. Susan looked perplexed, fully expecting to see her twelve-year-old son, not a naked little boy in Harold's arms. Noah looked exhausted, as though he had just come from an endless car ride and was now being carried off to bed.

"What are you talking about? Who is this?" But just

as she was mouthing these words Susan simultaneously recognized her son from a different era, a time of tenderness, a time of infatuation with Mom to the exclusion of all rivals. She clearly recognized him now, her Noah.

"But where did he come from and how did this happen?" Susan demanded to know. Harold wrapped a crocheted blanket they kept on the sofa around the boy as he drifted off to sleep. He explained how Mulligan became Noah, sparing her the more gruesome details. Neither could quite believe it. "The curse," Susan remembered. "This was the witch's hex, the punishment for killing her cat." Harold nodded, then asked as if to no one in particular, "So what do we do now?"

"If the witch could turn Noah into a cat, and the cat into a five-year-old Noah, then surely she can return Noah to his proper age," Susan surmised. "We must find her."

Harold pondered Susan's assertion for a while and then said, "But maybe we don't want to return Noah to his proper age."

"What are you saying, Harold?"

"Susan, don't you get it? We have a second chance. All the mistakes we made with Noah never happened. We can do it all over again, but this time, the right way." Susan's face blanched. Harold's suggestion was, well, unnatural.

"And what do we tell our family and what about all of Noah's friends?" Susan protested.

"I don't know...I don't know what to tell them...."

Harold was overwhelmed by his own suggestion. "We'll tell them the truth," Harold offered, "about the curse."

"Which curse are you talking about, Harold? The witch's curse...or ours?" "Ours?" Harold asked, dumbfounded.

"We have always been so sure we caused Noah unnecessary heartache because we did what we thought was best and more often than not, we were wrong. That curse. Now you want us to undo all that, but if we do, we won't have the same Noah. Our Noah will indeed be lost forever." Susan's tears dried and she spoke with the conviction and clarity of maternal love and good sense. Harold, feeling ashamed, embraced her.

Harold and Susan put their five-year-old Noah to bed and walked to their neighbor's house. Somehow, they knew the witch would be home. And indeed, before they even rang the bell, she appeared at the door. She looked less harsh than Susan remembered.

"My wife and I: we are so sorry about your cat," Harold said. Susan, in tears, nodded her agreement.

The witch looked at Harold, then at Susan. After a long pause, the witch looked up and said, "My name is Olivia."

"I am Susan."

"And I am Harold."

They had lived next door to this woman for years and now realized they had not even known her name.

"And your children?" the witch asked.

"Amanda and Noah."

"Yes, Noah." Her tone revealed the witch somehow knew this child had worried Susan and Harold even before the curse. The same tone exposed an unexpected empathy for the parents which prompted her to reverse the curse. Although the witch could be nasty, she was not heartless.

"Please, can you return our son to his current age?" Harold asked. And Susan, looking at the crone with pleading eyes, pressed her hands together as if in prayer.

The witch stared blankly. Harold and Susan's heart stopped. Finally, she said: "Go home. All will be well in the morning. You have my word." She gave them a sad but gentle smile.

Harold and Susan went home, as the witch had advised. For the first time in months, maybe years, they slept soundly, facing each other instead of the walls of their bedroom. The curse was over at last: of that they felt sure.

The Boys of Bedford Falls

Jude knew that with donations plummeting, the Southern Human Rights Project (SHRP), head-quartered in Jackson, Mississippi, could only afford to keep one senior lawyer, and Jude was hoping it would be Ben. Ben was Jude's brilliant African American colleague who grew up poor on the South Side of Chicago and negotiated the Scylla and Charybdis of violence and racism along the way. Ben dedicated his career to voting rights, renter's rights, Jim Crow laws with new names, and a basketful of other important social causes. He and his wife of twenty years had one kid in college and one on his way. His wife worked but did not make nearly enough to support them. Besides, Jude knew that Ben had been sending money to his siblings for years to help them stay afloat. Ben was a good man and a talented attorney, full of energy and common sense.

Jude's passion for human rights was overdetermined. He was born and raised in Atlanta, to the son of a Southern Baptist Convention obstetrician and an elementary school teacher, both of whom gradually moved away from the Church and toward the Civil Rights movement in the sixties. They were not particularly attentive parents and seemed more wrapped up in their causes than in their only child. Jude felt their absence but eventually learned to be self-sufficient. Growing up, the lines between his needs and the greater good seemed blurred. Intuitively, he understood that a way to be close with his parents was to join in their causes.

Jude and Ben were close colleagues who had worked together for decades. Jude liked and respected Ben and the feelings were mutual. It's not that Jude did not like his job and felt fine to relinquish it. To the contrary. However, he felt clearing the decks for Ben to continue at SHRP was the right thing to do. It seemed hypocritical to Jude, a white man of privilege and means, to stand in Ben's way.

Jude's husband Alan was a like-minded social worker from New York City. They met through their activities in the Jackson area, grew close, and came out and moved in together. After decades in the South, Jude and Alan moved to New York City two years ago, after Alan inherited his family's penthouse apartment on Riverside Drive. Jude was working just as hard for SHRP now, remotely, from New York, as he had when he and Alan were living in Jackson.

"Did it ever occur to you that SHRP would prefer Ben to you?" interjected Alan, over coffee and sweet tea lemon cake the Saturday after learning about the planned job cuts.

Alan's question caused the pain of presumably long-buried biases to flare up, like an undigested gristle in his gut.

"Well Alan, I suppose you're right. They certainly could choose Ben over me." Jude now had to confront his arrogance and prejudice on top of his guilt. He took a swig of coffee as if to help move the gristle along.

It was getting close to Christmas and although Jude and Alan were not into observing many traditions, they both relished watching Frank Capras's It's a Wonderful Life, which they did religiously every year. Jude found the first airing of the season, a Saturday night several weeks before Christmas. As was their custom, Jude prepared dinner so it would be ready just in time for the start of the movie.

"Is there really anyone as self-sacrificing as George Bailey?" Jude asked rhetorically, busily moving from station to station in the kitchen in the late afternoon. "Alan, pass me the Burgundy for the chicken." Jude strongly identified with George's dilemma regarding achievement of personal goals versus taking care of others. "I read there was some evolutionary advantage to altruism and that's why this trait tenaciously persists in the human gene pool," Jude continued, trying to disguise the transparency of his dilemma regarding Ben.

Jude queried Alan more directly now, as he placed the coq au vin in the oven. "Take George Bailey. Lost his hearing when he saved his brother from drowning. Sacrificed his own dreams to become a civil engineer to carry on his dead father's legacy and protect his community from a corrupt megalomaniac. Cancelled his honeymoon and wedding gifts to save his civic-minded business. Let his brother off the family business hook so he could do what suited him. Jesus." Jude got up to turn the oven down to 350.

"It's just a movie, Jude," Alan retorted. "I'll set the table. Do you want the Dansk plates for your gourmet concoction?" The couple settled into their usual places on the sofa in the living room, just in time for the start of the film. There was a palpable excitement that accompanied the simple opening titles, with "Buffalo Gals" playing gayly in the background. Jude and Alan watched intently, enjoying their food and drink.

They watched the scene where George entered Mr. Gower's store and pressed down on the peculiar cigar lighter. Alan recited young George's words along with George: "Hot dog, I wish I had a million dollars!" Jude smiled. The two enjoyed showing off their intimate knowledge of the movie script.

An hour later, Jude noticed that Alan was nodding off. "No more wine for you," Jude half-scolded in a louder than usual voice certain to wake him up. "Don't you think George got a bit of a raw deal, you know, looking back on his life realizing so many of his dreams would never come true?"

"No," Alan responded while yawning. "George had a loving wife, kids, and the satisfaction of helping others. And besides, you don't always get everything you want in life. You need to appreciate what you have." This was familiar territory for Alan when Jude got this way.

"It's a Christmas movie, for God's sake. Let it alone."

As the film drew to a close, Jude exclaimed with unrestrained sarcasm. "And it all comes together in that last scene, doesn't it. A bell ornament on the Christmas tree rings, Clarence the misfit angel gets his wings, they sing Aude Lange Syne, and all is well with the world. Except George still didn't get to do what he wanted to do." Jude paused, awaiting Alan's response, but there was none. "Do you think he woke up the next morning feeling satisfied...or the next year, for that matter?" Jude was almost yelling, relentlessly torpedoing the message of the film.

Alan was quiet now and Jude sensed he was irritated with his criticism of the movie, especially Jude's projected complaints on behalf of George. Jude noticed, too, that the movie he loved so much, that typically left him watery-eyed, had little effect this year, except to make him feel confused and a bit disillusioned.

Jude and Alan cleared the coffee table in near silence, washed the dishes, and went to bed.

"I'm thinking of resigning," Jude told Alan after a sleepless night, putting the pan of ricotta frittatas he'd made for their breakfast on a vintage Hamilton Beach hot plate. He needed to hear himself say it.

"You're what?" said Alan. "Are you out of your mind?"

"You know the situation," Jude went on. He served Alan, then himself. He poured them each some orange juice. "I may be let go anyway. But if it's Ben that gets tossed..."

"If it is? Then that's that. It's management's decision, not yours."

"I know. But ..."

"Christ, Jude, how did you even get this way? ..."

"Alan, I just can't see it any other way."

"Listen Jude, with all due respect to George Bailey, in the real world there are only two reasons people look out for the other guy before looking out for themselves. And evolution ain't one of them. Either they crave people's adoration and praise for being so damn selfless..."

Jude glared at Alan, trying to assimilate every word of the accusation that his concern for Ben was little more than a need for approval. "Or...," Jude blurted out, feeling his face flush with rage.

"Or...they feel undeserving."

Alan's words stopped Jude in his tracks. Jude's expression changed slowly but deliberately from disbelief and anger to comprehension and shame. He felt a loneliness and a yearning he had not felt since boyhood.

"So that's it, is it?" Jude uttered, half questioning, half understanding. He pictured George Bailey's crestfallen expression at the Bedford Falls train station at the moment he understood he must stay in town to carry on with the family business so his brother could accept a plumb job in Rochester. He could see himself doing precisely what George did. He was planning to do it now with Ben.

Alan embraced Jude and kissed his forehead, his lips gently nudging the truth into his brain. Jude appreciated Alan's affection but knew it could not begin to fill the void created by too little love spawning feelings of too little lovability.

"Alan," Jude uttered just above a whisper, his voice quivering, his left foot shaking uncontrollably. "It's very hard for me to see it any other way." Like the Loch Ness monster, Jude's revelation sparked by Alan's words barely poked its head above the surface before it again disappeared into the depths. Was it even real?

In the end, more out of paralysis than conviction, Jude allowed the decision process to proceed without offering his resignation. He would live with the resolution either way. Jude continued his work from home in the coming days, interacting with Ben via email as they always had. Although each man suspected their relationship would be changing soon, neither spoke of it. The email from the CEO came to both Ben and Jude on a Friday morning. The CEO would be arranging a Zoom meeting with each of them for later that day.

Jude's meeting was set for 12 PM. Apprehensive, he joined the meeting with his boss. "Jude, thanks for meeting with me today. I won't beat around the bush..." Jude knew the rest. The meeting with the CEO went on for several more minutes, but Jude was not present for most of it.

The meeting was over, and the decision was made, but Jude had trouble assimilating the outcome. He loved his job and would miss it dearly but also felt relieved that the burden of decision had been lifted. That evening, when Alan returned home from work, Jude gave him the news. "You did the right thing letting them decide. No need to stick your own head in the noose." Alan offered in loving gesture.

"I think I will go for a walk along the water," Jude said matter-of-factly.

"Would you like some company?" Alan asked.

"No thanks. I'm ok. Just want to stretch my legs," Jude replied.

Jude slowly gathered himself, along with his peacoat and wool hat. He walked out of his apartment to the elevator and pushed the down button. The elevator arrived, and the doors opened with the customary ringing of the bell he had heard hundreds of times. Jude entered, smiled faintly, and without turning around, realized he could move on despite the wall in front of him. "Atta boy, Clarence. That's right...that's right!"

Kippot

*L*eon tossed, frisbee-like, a blue satin *kippah* across the dining room. The skullcap, inscribed with Daniel and Rachel's Wedding, June 1, 1991, caromed off the credenza and into a plastic trash bin below.

"Leon, what are you doing?"

"Decluttering," Leon said as though he were recycling yesterday's Times.

Margie noted the piles of *kippot* on the dining room table and strained to see if any were burnt orange, relics of their own wedding fifty-one years before.

"Are you allowed to just throw them away?"

"No law against it. Checked with the rabbi. I'm fed up with having to pick them up off the floor every time I open the breakfront cabinet."

Margie paused, appearing confused. "How are you deciding which to keep and which to discard?"

"Degrees of separation." Leon had anticipated his wife's question. Margie raised her brow.

15 Original version published in the Macrame Literary Journal May, 2025

"The more distant the relationship, the more likely to get tossed." Her brow relaxed.

Margie picked up a canary yellow *kippah* from the table and read the inscription. "So, Bat Mitzvah of Sue Ellen Goldstein, a middle school friend of our Em...il...y..." Margie drew out her daughter's name as her fingers interrogated the adjacent piles. "Ah...here we are...would be tossed in favor of..." she squinted to read the faded letters..."Bar Mitzvah of Mark Stewart Glazer, your first cousin's son?"

"Exactly."

"Any other considerations?"

"Well, esthetics count. I like the colorful, hand-woven *kippot* from Guatemala and may keep some of those. On the other hand, *kippot* with a sports logo...straight to the bin."

"Have you had to make any tough calls yet?" Margie half-smirked.

"Interesting you should ask. I threw away In Honor of the Wedding of Harry and Sophie Saposnik, March 5, 1966."

"You didn't."

"They're dead fifteen years, at least. What's the point?"

"Leon, they were my favorite aunt and uncle. What will I have to remember them?"

"I guess, nothing...anymore. Sorry." Leon wasn't entirely sincere. Margie sighed.

"Have you considered donating them to a shul or recycling them?"

"When I asked the rabbi about donation, he offered to show me his stash.

"And what about the Goodwill?"

"Ah. Why didn't I think of that? There must be thousands of homeless in need of inscribed *kippot*." Leon emphasized his point by flinging In honor of Scott Rosenberg's Bar Mitzvah, January 2, 1999 across the table, just missing Margie's head. Blue suede with a Yankees insignia.

"OK. You made your point."

"There is one other consideration." Leon pointed to a grouping of *kippot* at the far end of the dining room table, some with inscription side up, some side down.

"What are those?"

"I call them my radioactive *kippot*. They need special handling; the *kippot* of divorces, of bat mitzvah girls who wandered off the path, or worse."

"Worse?"

Leon sprang up, waving his hands. He grabbed a

random *kippah* from the radioactive pile. "In Honor of Susan and Jeffrey Levy's Wedding...Suzy...cancer... dead." Then another, "Bar Mitzvah of Mark Berman...nervous breakdowns, in and out of mental hospitals." Leon motioned to hurl Mark's *kippah* toward the trash bin but returned it to the table instead. "They never saw it coming. How could they know?"

"Leon, is there something you want to tell me?"

"What do you mean?"

"Why are you all of sudden so concerned about our glut of *kippot*?"

"I don't know. It just feels like it's time."

"Time for what?"

"I want to be organized. Just in case."

"In case you die? It's not like packing a bag and waiting for a bus."

"Isn't it? I don't want to be snuck up on."

"Can't be changed."

"I know. I read all the inscriptions. The radioactive ones leave me cold. The others? Each one is a world. Who attended the wedding. The tumult. What I wore. What you wore. What Shelly Glickstein looked like in 1992 at her bat mitzvah. Stupid, stupid things." Leon began to sob.

Margie walked to her husband past the mounds of *kippot*; the white ones, the velvet ones, the leather ones, the gray, the maroon, the pastel pink, each with inscriptions that would someday, if not already, share language with gravestones. She slowly lowered herself onto his lap.

"Wait here."

She retreated to the kitchen, returned with a black Sharpie, and proceeded to inscribe the inside of a burnt orange *kippah*, In Honor of Margie and Leon's Decluttering Day, December 20, 2021.

"Here." Margie returned to her place on Leon's lap. He barely felt her weight.

Leon read the new inscription, placed the burnt orange *kippah* on his head, and gently kissed his bride.

Dry Run

The cyclic squeak of the rusted casket carriage was interrupted by the rabbi stopping.

"We pause every few steps," she said, "so as not to make this last journey seem easy or efficient."

Motionless, like the other pall bearers, all of us men, I held the casket rail tightly with both hands. I did not look up from the coffin even when the procession resumed. My seventy-year-old frame was struggling despite the rabbi's respites. The gravedigger directly ahead of me guided the carriage by the handle. His body odor mixed with the smell of hot matted grass and made me queasy as we baked under the noon sun.

An hour earlier in the funeral home I recalled staring at the casket and thinking, "It doesn't seem so bad." A lifetime earlier, as a child, I would cross the street to avoid walking in front of such places.

Sitting in the air-conditioned chapel, I pictured myself lying in the box, an inch-thick pad underneath my body. I was wearing sweatpants, a T-shirt, and white gym socks without shoes. I had a comforter pulled up under my chin the way I liked it when I slept, even during the summer. I could detect the faint aroma of a cold fireplace the morning after the logs had burned out. Joni Mitchell's Blue album was in my head, vinyl, playing over and over. And the pleasing anticipation of something great to look forward to, like my first train set, or my first "my body's yours," flooded my mind. I imagined that's the way it would be.

The rabbi walked on. The casket jerked forward almost trapping my foot under the front wheel. Friedman. Weiss. Sorokin. Past the backs of headstones, I wondered what each said on the front; "Beloved Father and Grandfather," "Devoted Wife, Woman of Valor." My mind wandered to less conventional possibilities; "Her Brisket was to Die For," "He Was Always Right."

We approached the grave. The edges were lined with four two-by-six wooden planks, and the empty hole was straddled by a tarnished silver casket-lowering device with two green straps positioned between cylindrical pullies.

"Now be careful here. Come towards me. A little more...turn...use both hands...keep turning...lower the casket... gently.... gently." The gravedigger who had led our entourage across the rutted turf between rows of monuments now functioned as a boatswain, coaxing us to safely moor the boat.

"Whoa!" My foot slipped into a hidden gap between the wooden plank and the edge of the pit. I frantically pulled it back and swept the dirt from my trouser leg.

"Mind the gap." The gravedigger slyly shot me a smile. He seemed to be the only one to notice my mishap. "It's an omen," he said, as his smile dissolved.

"Stand back," the gravedigger ordered. Without uttering a word, he curled his finger, motioning to co-workers who seemed to appear from nowhere. They released the pulleys with perfect coordination and lowered the coffin to the bottom of the grave. The actions were so well practiced as to avoid the expected thump on hitting bottom. The only sound was that of dense fabric rubbing against mahogany, the straps briskly retracted like slurped spaghetti.

"Please step forward if you wish to assist in the burial." The rabbi instructed the gathered to first use the back of the shovel blade to signify reluctance in completing the task.

"And as we cover the casket let us remember that to do so is the greatest mitzvah in our tradition. It is the only mitzvah that can never be repaid." The rabbi continued the recitation of a psalm in an undertone.

Still preoccupied with the residue on my pants, I

watched as two lines formed and each attendee did their duty. The sounds of fine-grained soil, clumps of loam held together with tenacious blades of grass, and the occasional stone echoed from the lid of the casket. Each missile elicited its own distinctive sound. Dissonance was all the noises had in common. The harsh reverberations grew muted, replaced by the dullness of dirt on dirt as the mourners filled the grave.

"Be sure to cover each corner of the casket!" The rabbi's tone as she interrupted her prayer was itself mildly dissonant.

One of the burlier pall bearers, shovel in hand, obeyed.

"That's good," the rabbi said, then looked at me, still picking dirt from my trousers. "The Mourner's Kaddish usually comes next. Perhaps we should stop the service here."

"Stop?" I asked.

The rabbi nodded.

"Yes...fine, fine..." I skimmed the gathering with clipped glances. "I don't want to cross the line."

"No. There's only so far we can go with an empty casket."

About the Author

Dr. Mark Russ was born in Cuba, the son of Yiddish-speaking Holocaust survivors, blue collar laborers with little formal education. He grew up in a lower middle-class neighborhood in Philadelphia, Pennsylvania and attended public schools, including Central High School where he was Editor-in-Chief of the school's literary magazine and recipient of several English prizes.

Dr. Russ received his BA with High Honors in Biology in 1976 from Haverford College and his MD from Drexel University College of Medicine in 1980 with Academic Distinction in Mental Health Sciences. He completed his internship, residency, and chief residency in Psychiatry at Montefiore Einstein College of Medicine in 1984. He joined the faculty of New York-Presbyterian Westchester Behavioral Health in 1984, where he assumed positions of increasing clinical and administrative responsibility

Dr. Russ moved to the Zucker Hillside Hospital/Northwell in 1996 where he was the Director of Acute Care Psychiatry. At the Zucker Hillside Hospital, Dr. Russ was the director of inpatient and emergency services for most of his eighteen-year tenure, and Associate Professor of Psychiatry at the Zucker School of Medicine at Hofstra/Northwell.

In 2015, Dr. Russ returned to New York-Presbyterian where he was Vice Chair and Medical Director of New York-Presbyterian Westchester Behavioral Health and Professor of Clinical Psychiatry at Weill Cornell Medical College. In 2023, Dr. Russ moved on to his current role of Chief Medical Officer at Silver Hill Hospital in New Canaan, Connecticut.

Dr. Russ' academic interests have included exploring the neurobiological underpinnings of self-injurious behavior in patients with borderline personality disorder, assessment of suicide risk, aggressive behavior in psychiatric inpatients, inpatient unit structure and function, quality improvement and the COVID-19 crisis. He has taught and mentored hundreds of psychiatric trainees throughout his career, and has received several teaching awards. He has authored forty-five peer-reviewed psychiatric papers and in 2025 released his book titled "The Family Guide to Psychiatric Hospitalization" published by Johns Hopkins University Press.

Approximately five years ago, Dr. Russ began writing the short stories contained in the current collection. Fifteen of these stories have been published in online literary magazines including *Sortes, Bright Flash Literary Review, Literally Stories, Macrame Literary Journal, Jewishfiction.net, The Concrete Desert Review, Jimson Weed, The Jewish Writing Project, Blue Lake Review, FigTreeLit, Of The Book, BooksNPieces,* and *The Minison Project.*

www.ingramcontent.com/pod-product-compliance
Lightning Source LLC
Chambersburg PA
CBHW050258110726
47898CB00007B/2453